"The most powerful writing yet from Gibbons."

—*San Antonio Express-News*

"One of her best. . . . On almost every page, Kaye Gibbons enlivens her story with surprising turns of phrase, striking images, and sharp observations."

—*Baltimore Sun*

"Gibbons's sentences are . . . wonderfully lucid and lyrical at once."

—*Chicago Tribune*

"[H]earkens back to the Brontë sisters. Gibbons's tale is atmospheric and unsettling, narrated in hushed Victorian tones and ornamented with period flourishes."

—*Publishers Weekly*

"It is vintage Gibbons gorgeously written, filled with insights about women and memorable characters." —Newhouse News Service

"With lean and graceful prose, Gibbons gives flesh to the meanings of love and resilience and oppression and cruelty."

—*Memphis Commercial Appeal*

"[E]minently readable, with smooth flowing sentences that draw the reader in. . . . [S]ilky prose and social portraiture make it a work of grace and intelligence. . . . All readers who appreciate fine writing will enjoy it."

—*Richmond Times-Dispatch*

DIVINING WOMEN

Kaye Gibbons

HARPER
PERENNIAL

A hardcover edition of this book was published in 2004 by G. P. Putnam's Sons, a member of Penguin Putnam Inc. It is here reprinted with arrangement with Penguin Group (USA) Inc.

P.S.™ is a trademark of HarperCollins Publishers Inc.

FIRST HARPER PERENNIAL EDITION PUBLISHED 2005.

Designed by Amanda Dewey

The Library of Congress has catalogued the hardcover edition as follows:

Gibbons, Kaye.
Divining women : a novel / Kaye Gibbons. p. cm.
    "A Marian Wood book."
    ISBN 0-399-15160-5
    1. Women—North Carolina—Fiction.
    2. North Carolina—Fiction. 3. Married women—Fiction.
    4. Abused wives–Fiction. 5. Young women–Fiction.
    6. Influenza—Fiction. I. Title.
    PS3557.I13917D585   2003   2003060661
    813'.54—dc22

ISBN-10: 0-06-076028-1 (pbk.)
ISBN-13: 978-0-06-076028-1 (pbk.)

05 06 07 08 09 ❖/RRD 10 9 8 7 6 5 4 3 2 1

ACKNOWLEDGMENTS

I know that I've sometimes made empty though convincing promises that some individuals could win a spot on these pages in exchange for things like faster printing service, deeper bakery discounts, a hotel room with a view of the park. However, I was always in a hurry and never kept a list. While I feel awful about it, there is nothing to be done now, and I can only hope that those kind, compliant people do not read this book or even learn of its existence. But there are some things for which no list is required, as I am reminded of certain words and acts of goodwill every few minutes of the day.

During one especially laborious phase of this writing process, I called my agent and threatened to find a real job. I could be a prison guard or bottle soda pop, for the daily terror and repetitive drudgery of both jobs seemed in line with what was being required of me right then. Liz said, "Nobody wants you to fail. We love you." It was as necessary a thing as I had ever heard.

"We" are the people who have wished me well during this process and embraced my daughters and me at every turn. I want to thank Barbara, David, and Michael Batts for encouraging responsible eccentricity; John David Batts for reading my mind and carrying me down Lexington Avenue and beyond; Professor William E. Leuchtenburg for making me see humanity in history; Sandy and Winston Page for their example of love; Lewis Black for his feat of revitalization; Jim Wolcott for his kind wisdom; Irv Coates for the odor of his grand Reader's Corner in Raleigh; Anna Jardine for her hard work; Liz Darhansoff for her steady guidance; and my editor, Marian Wood, smart, driven, honest. That "we" has cheered me along in various ways, and I thank Michael Gibbons, Amy Tan, Bart O'Connor, John Grisham, Chuck and Katherine Frazier, Barry Moser, Stella Connell, Jane Pasanen, Judith Lawson, Lee Smith, Susan Gladen, Susan Ketchin, Oscar Hijuelos, Chuck Verrill, Nancy Olson, Jan Taylor, John and Mel Evans, Susanne Marrs, Dr. Lewis Thorpe, Nancy Stafford, Tony Reevy, Oprah Winfrey, Winston and Ann Clinton Groom, Morris Dees, Jo Ann Pritchard Morris, Will and Becky McKee, Bro and Danny Williams, Pat Conroy, Harley Easter, June Crain, Mimi Rogers, Joan Micklin Silver, Doug and Melinda Marlette, Susan May Pratt, Ken Mitchell, Bernie and Katie Reeves, Mary Edna Williams, Mary Ann

Kahn, my sister Alice, and my aunt Jeanette Bloodworth, whose suggestion that we start our own religion will always amaze me.

I think of Eudora Welty, who recited a poem to me from her memories of how the Great Flu Epidemic of 1918 affected her town and her family. She said, "It goes, 'I had a little bird, his name was Inza. I opened the window, and in-flew-Inza.' You ought to use that in your book. That's how they helped explain to the little children about death. You see, there was so much of it."

And there seemed to be so much of it while this novel was being written. Faith Sale, my editor and closest friend, Willie Morris, Joseph Heller, Tim McLaurin, Al Braselton, and dear Jeanne Braselton. After September 11, I wrote harder, moving the novel in a new, darker direction, for these shocks of mortality had made anything less feel like just that. I honor the people, living and gone, who made this long journey possible. In my life I've loved them all.

I even have a superstition that has grown on me as the result of invisible hands coming all the time—namely, that if you follow your bliss you put yourself on a kind of track that has been there all the while, waiting for you, and the life that you ought to be living is the one you are living. When you can see that, you begin to meet people who are in the field of your bliss, and they open the doors to you. I say, follow your bliss and don't be afraid, and doors will open where you didn't know they were going to be.

Have you ever had sympathy for the man who has no invisible means of support?

Who has no invisible means? Yes, he is the one that evokes compassion, the poor chap. To see him stumbling around when all the waters of life are right there really evokes one's pity.

The waters of eternal life are right there? Where?

Wherever you are—if you are following your bliss, you are enjoying that refreshment, that life within you, all the time.

JOSEPH CAMPBELL,
The Power of Myth

DIVINING WOMEN

Prologue

September 12, 1939

The woman I loved was rushed into the arms of grace this morning, sometime close to dawn. I had her pulled into me, and she was curved, rounded, as though she was folding into herself, back down into a quiet and softly familiar womb. I could feel the sharp bones of her spine through her fragile skin and the layers of flannel that I had hoped would protect her and keep her warm—the discomfort of her raw skin and cold bones and the joy of a few vagrant, roaming memories were all that was left by then, by midnight, that seemed to bind her to this place. Her name was Maureen. And with the memories that came unbound, unloosened with her flight, I am still beside her, now.

One

I climbed aboard the Carolinian at Union Station on September 10, 1918, at seven o'clock in the morning, and within minutes we were out of the tunnel and moving southward in a level, determined rush. In fifteen hours, I would be in Elm City, North Carolina, where I was to be a sort of temporary lady's companion to my expectant aunt Maureen, a woman I had never met in the five years she had been married to my mother's half brother, Troop Ross. Their first child was due in November. I had never met my uncle, either, but I had heard about him all my life. My mother had been able to keep up a loose, tentative connection with him, as she was always merrily impervious to insult. Maureen had been only a figure in the background of the marriage, remembered fondly and greatly pitied.

Troop's mother had been my grandfather Toby Greene's first wife. She had jerked the boy out of Washington when he was eight and taken him to her family's home in North Carolina, so angry and repulsed by her husband's new pet hobby, nudism, that she denied him any contact with his son and also dropped his name. From what my family gathered, she let people assume that he had died. She was locally admired for her well-bred, stoic refusal to go into any detail, and her sadistically critical and smothering child-rearing tactics were interpreted as the hectic attentiveness of a lonely widow, trying to do the best she could to raise her boy alone.

Her tastefully concealed rage and obsession never abated. From her departure in 1875 to her death in 1911, she hounded and taunted my grandfather and his second wife, Leslie, through the mails, demanding that the two of them rot from some "fanny disease" she hoped they would catch while romping naked in the woods, demanding that they then die of the inborn selfishness that she believed had initially compelled Toby to go off on a tangent and humiliate her. But despite her morbid hopes and wishes for him and his new wife, which eventually expanded to include my mother, Martha, their only child, she let them know that she and Troop deserved and expected to be supplied with the best of everything in exchange for Toby's having flitted off and made a mockery of her honor and her marriage by joining the American Community of Nudists, among other "sinister organizations." She subscribed to the Washington morning and afternoon papers by post so that she could keep herself and her son educated about family activities, and would fire off commentary whenever anything about the Greenes appeared.

Oftentimes, in the same letter that contained a bitter indictment of Toby and his family as freethinking freaks or idiots who had chosen to squander the excellent address and socially privileged position they so fortunately inherited, she would insist that Toby promptly finance a wild range of entitlements beyond the generous annuities, incomes, and trusts he had already settled upon her. After he married again in 1876, and when my mother was born a year later, when she married in 1895, and on the occasion of my birth, in 1896, the letters were more incredible than usual. She blistered the lot of us, including me, "that new infant who has no doubt been issued a massive silver spoon by her doting grandfather," in a crazed preface to her catalogue of insatiable demands for protracted stays in Europe, oceanfront suites at The Breakers in Palm Beach, Louis Vuitton trunks, and dresses from Doucet and Worth. My grandfather was ignorant with regard to the luggage and the dresses, but the women in the family were not. Despite their own frugality, one of their favorite pastimes was looking at the fashion magazines, and when they went to New York, they stayed at the Waldorf-Astoria and enjoyed watching the elegant ladies parading up and down Peacock Alley. After they explained the clothing request to my grandfather, how these dresses tended to be worn by the ultra-ultra set, how much they cost, he shouted out loud, "My God! Nora is too far too broad for that kind of merchandise!"

But she was determined to make him pay for, as she described it, one day marrying her in high Episcopal style, with the promise of including her in the exquisite Washington society he had always known, and then announcing, right after "that strange honeymoon trip to India, of all places," that he was now ready to explore some nontraditional interests he had been hoarding. The nudism was certainly the worst of it, but she was also angry that he could not simply be satisfied with the vision of the two of them floating forever on a river of inherited family money. By her lights, he could work in the mornings, managing investments, have lunch at a club, and then come home and tell her how handsome she looked in her new clothes. She had everything sorted out.

When my grandfather explained that he had not duped or misled her, she would not let herself understand that he was only searching for an identity beyond his family's wealth and position. He could not make her see that he would be a happier man if he could satisfy his vivid curiosity and that they were both blessed that he had the means to do it while keeping her beautifully clothed and shod. He told me that he explained a hundred times in a hundred ways that they could each do everything they wanted to do, individually and together, that he had realized how unfair it was for one of them to wither while the other thrived. When he showed me what my family called "the trove," the crate containing more than three hundred letters, which I read after my mother had decided I was going to North Carolina, I asked him why he had taken a young bride with such worldly sensibilities to India, even if he had promised her five trips to London to make up for it. What he told me about that trip, as well as the rest of the marriage, helped explain why my family always regarded the confluence of love and freedom as an elemental requirement of life.

"I wanted to see what they thought mattered in Calcutta," he told me. "And it turned out not to be whether the fricassee was prepared right. So many things made an impress on me. Manners meant dignity and not causing another person pain. But I was certainly causing my new wife pain. Poor thing, she hated it, and hated me for taking her. I was leaving her asleep in the mornings and walking out to the river and weeping. I wished I'd found out everything I did before I married her, but we all learn what we need at the right time, when we can bear the news. If she and I had been able to let one another be, things would have worked out differently."

The last letter she wrote him was dated May 5, 1911. Troop was forty-four, and she spoke of him as though he were thirteen. After I had read it, I took it to my grandfather and asked whether I should perhaps find something else to do in these months that had become open for me, whether I should leave my uncle alone and write a nice note wishing my aunt the best.

"I'll be going," I told him, "into the home of the boy this woman created."

"Oh," he said, "it's worse than that. He is the man she created."

May 5, 1911

Dear Tobias,

Happy 35th Anniversary! And how is that amusing little wife of yours who had the temerity to sign that birthday check for my son? Is something wrong that you cannot sign your own name these days? Are you in jail because you've finally been arrested on a morals charge?

Congratulations as well on your picture being in the paper, raising money at a gala affair for some "cause," to which you had given a pretty penny. A piece of advice—a gentleman would pay more attention that his wife's clothing looks well on her. But I forgot that you two are above caring about that kind of thing. Speaking of which, I failed to compliment you when you had Mrs. Teddy Roosevelt in the house, enjoying helping Miss Leslie make persimmon preserves in her "homey kitchen." Did you invite her, or did she just instinctively know to come because your home is such a social magnet?

It has been 36 years since you caused me to leave, and I left under the impression that if I stayed, it would have meant not being able to do nice things and participate in life, and I have counted nine times that you and Miss Leslie or your strange housemates, Leonard and Louise Oliver, have had your pictures in the paper. There have been fifty-one mentions of these names and twelve of your "splendid" daughter Martha. Do you know how unseemly that is?

Despite your neglect of your son, you can trust that I have tried to be a good accompanist to his social and professional career. And as deprived as my son and I have been while you and your other family have been having it both ways and being naked in the woods one night and in evening clothes at an embassy affair the next, we've been happier than I could have ever imagined. Although we've been forced to live in Elm City, North Carolina, amongst people whose pathetic local social aspirations we had to adapt to if were to enjoy going around in any society at all, we have been beloved and recognized as people of quality and worth.

What is needed right now is that my son and I recover from this anniversary that you so blithely celebrate, and I think I should like to take him to Europe this summer to do it. I need to give the company a deposit in ten days. It should not be too much more than it was last year, but I cannot be held accountable for the rise in the modern cost of living.

Sincerely,

Nora Worthy Ross

As she was writing that dunning letter, one of the few people in Elm City, North Carolina, who had more money than she was her son. Despite her portrayal of him as a shocked child, barely hanging on to his senses because of all these problems of doing without, triggered by his selfish father's wedding anniversary, he was a responsible and trusted businessman, in one of the chief vice-presidential positions at the American Tobacco Company. It had been his lack of scholarship rather than of money that sent him to a small college close to his mother that cost my grandfather as much as

Harvard would have. In one of her letters, written while Troop was only thirty minutes by train from his mother, she blamed Grandfather Toby not only for her heartache but also for the fall of Western civilization, because had her son been able to attend Harvard and enter one of the professions, even the clergy, he would have been better equipped to "win the Presidency and uplift fallen standards the world over, but no." Again, Nora would not accept the truth. Grandfather Toby had not attended college at all. He had read law with a district judge, although he never practiced it. He was not in a position to influence Troop's admission to Harvard or anywhere else, but she behaved as though providing him that kind of access were merely another prerogative of both his social station and his guilt, and she was relentless about it. He was once telling me how guilty he had felt for years that he had not been equipped to provide his son with a good college, when Mother walked in. It was difficult for her to watch him rummaging around in his memory for a way he could have made everything right.

Mother told me, "Mary, I want you to hear what I have told my father a dozen times, something he cannot quite accept, because guilt tends to get in the way of his reason. I know I sound angry, but I am only aggravated that a man who has found this wonderful, authentic way to live, who has brought his family nothing but joy, has had to contend with this niggling persecution. Nothing he could have done would have changed anything. I grew up watching him carry this blame, not just about Harvard. The two of them should look to themselves. What they would see is an intellectually lazy individual who would not touch a book unless it contained instructions for his own advancement, and a mother who has told him that he is owed the world, though actually earning it would be common. And they have developed a very different notion of what normal means. It is not our fault that they fantasize that we move about in some nonexistent splendid existence. The two of them create their own problems. They think that my father has done nothing. I know he's done too much. The only thing he did not do is give Troop a sound whipping, and that, I can say from having raised your brother, was what was needed most of all."

In 1894, after the papers ran an article that celebrated the "High Sights" of female high school graduates, including my mother, a letter soon arrived in which Nora expressed absolute glee over finally having vindicated her son's remarkable failure. She confused Barnard College with Miss Porter's in an ignorant forecast of "young Martha's sad inability to realize her much-trumped promise by having to attend one of these holding schools for society cows." She hoped that my mother was grateful for the money available to groom her to properly breed. But Nora never attacked my mother directly. She sent nothing but flowers and ordinary, courteous cards to her when my father and brother died. She was justifiably intimidated by the restrained self-assurance that my mother showed in being able to contact her half brother a few times each year without mentioning to either of them the trove of correspondence.

When Mother went down to North Carolina, for Nora's funeral, she took a note her father had written for his son.

"But," Mother told me later, "a remarkable thing happened. I noticed a stunningly beautiful woman at the funeral and the cemetery. She had come by herself. It became clear that the two of them were together. It looked as if he had waited for his mother to be in the ground before he touched her— which he did all right. He leaned on her heavily, touched her neck and cried on her shoulder. It was a strange sight. She was very tall and dark, almost Italian-looking, and him so pale with his white hair combed back."

Mother waited for him to walk away before she went over to meet the woman. Her name was Maureen Carlton, and she was originally from Yazoo City, Mississippi, where she met Troop when he was in the Delta on business. She had moved to North Carolina and taken a clerical job at the tobacco company two years before, early in 1909. Mother said that she seemed nice, and this baffled and intrigued her, given Troop's character. To avoid any complications that might arise from the lie that had been so dramatically lived in North Carolina, Mother introduced herself to people as an old friend of the family. When Maureen heard this, she discreetly responded that Troop had told her about the family situation in Washington, and said she was sorry, as it sounded hard for everyone. Mother was taken aback to learn that although the woman had heard Nora's praises sung for two years, the first time she actually saw her was when she was in her coffin. And then Maureen took Mother's hand as she left the room, and said how dear it had been to meet her and how she looked forward to meeting other members of Troop's family, if not before then certainly at the wedding.

Two

I grew up around three women who did not ask permission before they offered me a view of their wide and deep universe, and even now, at forty-three, I still find that much of my outlook comes from a continuously looping reel of memories, and I am able to see and hear what they felt, thought, and did. When I have fallen, it has invariably been through the places they left for me to discover for myself. And when I have luxuriated in any reward of love or labor, even if I have every right to claim the accomplishment for myself, when enough layers of time are peeled away, there is always a scene of a lesson being taught, sometimes taken, sometimes not. But there is always a correspondence between the lesson and the reward.

My mother must have worked on my lesson plans the whole trip back from North Carolina, after Nora's funeral, although my grandmothers required no preparation. Because of the concerns that arose after Mother brought the news that my uncle was marrying a person who appeared stable and pulled together, with no obvious history as a mental patient, the three of them seemed to swivel around and see me, at fifteen, as suddenly vulnerable and in danger of being fooled, manipulated, and then abandoned by a man. Even from hundreds of miles away, they had decided that Maureen and Troop's incongruous match amounted to nothing more than the promise of misery for her and the threat of something similar for me.

After Mother reported on her initial impression of Maureen, she exiled the men from the house, explaining that the company of women was best for me now, but when they were gone, she said, "The truth is that my father is too tender-hearted to hear what his son did to me. What happened when I was alone with Troop after the funeral is in a different category entirely from anything he and his mother have ever sent our way. And I also could not tell him how much Maureen reminded me of you, Mary. You and she have the same trusting look on your face that tells people that you're more than likely going to believe anything they say. There were small things as well, the way you both stand and look out over a room, the way fabric fits you in the hips. But mainly it was the way she tilted her head and smiled as I spoke—it made me feel anyone could spot that open nature and step right in to take advantage of her."

Grandmother Louise said, "My theory is that she has some family money. Being from Mississippi, her father may own a plantation. Troop wants the slaves and the money."

Mother sighed and told her that plantations were merely large farms and did not require slaves to run them. "No, Maureen wasn't raised anywhere near any kind of money," she said. "Her family's poor."

When I told my mother how amazed I was that someone she'd just met would disclose something as awful as that, she replied, "No, she said nothing about it. Her fingernails did. They were ridged, furrowed, like garden rows." They knew, but I learned that this is an unmistakable indication of childhood malnourishment. Sadness for this stranger washed over me, and I needed to know more about her.

"Well," Mother said, "I said that she was tall. And she wore her clothes well on her body, which I know is an odd thing to say, but she did."

Grandmother Louise said, "What did she have on? Tell me. I'm interested. We can tell if she called this turmoil on herself."

Louise Canton Oliver was a tiny woman with lovely café-au-lait skin and such small hands and feet that she had to wear children's gloves and shoes. Her clothing had to be cut from little girls' patterns, but she would order only black fabrics, which absorbed heat and kept her pleasingly warm to the bone and also gave her the overall air of a deadly serious child. Although she had this unchanged and odd habit of dressing, she was the one who provided a running narration when we watched the ultra-ultra set parade at the Waldorf.

The current designs and trends were all familiar to her, and she was able to speak of them with an uncanny facility. We knew that if Mother could provide a thorough inventory of Maureen's clothing, my grandmother could give a fairly exacting analysis of her character and possibly even of why she was letting herself in for such trouble. It was my grandmother's chosen method of divination in a family that listened to the counsel of cards, fate boards, tea leaves, and ghosts, and I had long believed that she was far more reliable than these. Hers was the only authority that was left unquestioned, something that could not be said of the various temperamental prophets who were hired to give readings without first understanding that my family might debate and amend any unsuitable or inconvenient destinies.

Mother knew to begin with whether Maureen had chosen a plain or an ornate look on a day when she was presenting herself to a world of new people, this the most telling sign of an inherent presence or dearth of common sense. "My first impression," Mother said, "was that she was confident, full of practical intelligence, and capable of being a bit headstrong if she decided it was called for. Her stockings had a thin vine of wild flowers embroidered around the ankles, but not at all conspicuous. Seeing it was like finding a wonderful small gift, but I had the uneasy feeling that the women in Troop's crowd would say it was vulgar. The men wouldn't, but they didn't look like men who were allowed too many stray personal opinions, particularly about a beautiful woman like Maureen. Her dress was a black sleeveless shift, with sharp pleats at the waist, very modern, clean lines. I could tell by the seams that she'd made it, but it was still as professional a job as anyone is ever going to do at home. It'd take somebody with a fearless but exceedingly calm streak to look at four yards of raw silk spread out on the floor and not see that first cut leading to anywhere but thorough ruination."

Grandmother Louise said, "A poor woman who attacks an expensive piece of fabric by herself will tolerate more than most of us will, and for longer, but if her husband crosses her, he's eventually going to suffer."

The manner of Maureen's dress and carriage was adequate proof that she was not so lacking in self-worth that she needed Troop's admiration to thrive or exist. She trusted her own judgment, as she insisted on presenting a stylish individuality to a group of people to whom the safety of conformity and tradition meant almost everything. Troop must have treated her well thus far: Grandmother Louise was certain that she would've rejected him if he had once shown her the face we had all seen. If he had not, if he truly loved her and had demonstrated it with his words and deeds and not one accidental exposure of his capacity for wrath and delusional vengeance, then she could not be faulted for marrying him. She must have found it unusual that he waited for his mother to die to propose, and must have wondered why he maintained the battery of deceptions about his Washington relations, but she had already enfolded him with the same trust and anticipation of happiness that Mother had seen on her face and mine.

The only thing that any of us could do now was try to find in ourselves the same expectation that Maureen would be happy, that her husband would not turn on her the moment she became aware of the deceit. My mother's greatest fear was that a lie so large could not be maintained without fatigue and anxiety overwhelming their household. The first time that Maureen was tired or critical, distant, imperfect or human, he might recall the brutal price his mother exacted from him in exchange for her unconditional support. He might realize that he despised this woman he was trapped with as much as he despised his mother, his family, his world, anyone who selfishly expected him to give his love, concern, pleasure, and respect, the very emotions he believed he had to hoard for his own survival.

Mother said, "But then, Mary, I thought about those two boys who took you to the dances in January and March and left you alone to watch them having the time of their lives. I failed to see it coming either time. And I had been told all of my life to expect and look for signs and guidance everywhere, to search a person's face and listen to the voice and sort out the truth. So have you, Mary. We were both raised alert."

I must have looked puzzled, as Grandmother Leslie said, "What your mother means is that we have all enjoyed a different sort of emphasis on life from what most other people have seen, and she wishes it had served her better when she was feeding her cookies to those two young men she was entrusting you to, unchaperoned, before they snatched you off and stranded you. But what Louise and I can tell you is that these unnecessary little tragedies in a young woman's life will happen indefinitely, as long as people keep thinking that honor now means not running another individual over in your speedy automobile on the way to a job of work and back. In the last century, a young man's mother would've explained to him what an important responsibility it was to escort a young lady. He would've cut out his own tongue before he would've used it to tell her anything on the order of, 'Have a good time watching me dance with the other girls, and then hitch a ride home the best way you know how.'"

"It will never happen again," I told her, "and I appreciate the worry. But can we go on to the next part of the story? What did Uncle Troop do that was so ugly?"

The party episodes needed to stay in the background, where I had been trying to put them when I moved to the closet in the spare bedroom the dresses I had worn, so I would not have the daily reminder of their cost, the time and money my mother had spent on them. I would look at those two disappointed dresses and wonder how I could tell my mother that, for reasons I could not name, the experiences had not crushed me. Had there been words, I could've talked to her and saved her the weeks she spent trying to compensate for what the young men had done to me, all of her tender services, the tea cakes made, the books bought, the kind notes left on my dresser. I had been embarrassed at the first dance and mortified at the second, naturally, but I was not interpreting the evenings as the rehearsals for a long and lonely life.

My chief concern was that I was not actually suffering the way my mother was sure I was when I closed my bedroom door. And I was not nearly as unnerved or insulted as my grandmothers, who later cornered the mother of one of the "hoodlums" in the lobby of Ford's Theatre and suggested that the boy's home training had been "off," and that he present a diploma from an etiquette class if he ever came around my house again. When they reported that they had done this on my behalf, I thanked them and then listened to everyone praise my efficient recovery. I was unable to admit that I had felt like a foreigner during these discussions. When they listed the merits they required in a young man for me, I felt separate and apart, as though my heart was speaking a different language.

"Yes, now, being alone with Troop," Mother began. "No one can ever tell Father this part of the story. When Troop saw me with Maureen, he came right over and more or less guided me away into another room. When he closed the door, I told him that we were all sorry for his loss, and then I handed him Father's letter, saying only that he had wanted me to give it to him in person. Troop opened the envelope and, without reading the note card, squared the edges and tore both in half."

Grandmother Leslie said, "Did you think that Toby could not hear that his son destroyed a note because he saw that there was no check in it? You know your father is a bigger man than that."

"No," my mother said. "Listen to me. After he threw the pieces away, he spoke very calmly and quietly, and asked me to tell him exactly why I had told Maureen that he was my brother. I had not. He wanted to know why I felt entitled to come into his home on the day he buried his dear mother and spread lies about him, why I tried to tarnish his reputation by telling Maureen that everyone else in his family had refused to come. I had not done this, either. He said, 'You have a shocking amount of nerve to try and turn her against me. Do I look stupid enough to let you do it?'"

As fast as my heart was racing, I could not fathom being in my mother's position. I had been admiring the courage it took for her to attend the funeral, which she had done so that he could never claim to have been cut off by this family and because she believed it was the right and decent thing to do.

Mother went on: "I told him that I had said nothing, but I couldn't be held accountable for his imagination. I said, 'Troop, I've watched my family obey you and your mother my entire life. Our home has absorbed the hostility, but mercifully there's been enough goodness to overcome it. So, best wishes to you on the wedding, and my wish for that very nice young lady is that she opens her eyes sooner rather than later and sees what a sad, sad man you are.'"

We weren't sure whether my mother was telling us what she had said or what she had dreamed of saying. "If you actually said those things to that boy, God knows what he did when you got through," Grandmother Leslie told her. "Nora will show up and persecute us all if there was any kind of scene at her funeral."

"No, no more scenes," Mother said. "When I was leaving, he came outside and told me never to come back, never to contact him in any way whatsoever. He spat the words at my feet. I swore that I would, if he would do the same. I told him he obviously didn't need another dime from Washington, so both the emotional and the financial blackmail could stop. And our civility would extend only as far as birthday and holiday greetings—short, to the point, and nice.

"When he asked me if that was all, I told him that the only other thing I could ask for that was truly worth the petty and malicious aggravation was the promise that he would be a husband and one day perhaps a father who was as capable of sympathy and regret as his own father. When I calmed down enough to say he should feel welcome to send announcements of the wedding and of any other normal occasions in his new family's life, as long as they were civilized, I saw relief in his eyes for the second before he turned away. He stood facing the front door. He was not going to let me see his eyes, but when I called at his back, asking if he promised everything, he nodded that yes, he did."

Everyone was overwhelmed with gratitude at the thought of peace. But just as Mother spared her father the narration of the scene she had left that morning, she could not allow his heart to be broken if the vows were not kept. Mother was confident, but not convinced, as Troop's sense of entitlement was so extraordinary that he might decide the consequences either did not exist or were nothing in comparison with the benefits to be gained from continuing to lash out.

"So," she said, "we will wait and see, and when it feels safe, we will tell Father that the letter I gave to Troop worked, that his son agreed to try to see his mother's death as a reminder of how brief a time we all are given to take some pleasure from our lives."

"How did you know that the letter was a cease-and-desist

order?" Grandmother Louise asked. "You know I sympathize, but what did you do, steam it open?"

"No," Mother told us, smiling, "one thing I left out about meeting Maureen was that she was very accommodating. I told her I needed to use a pen and paper for a private matter, and she excused herself to find them, saying she should go ahead and start acquainting herself with where her mother-in-law had kept things. She said she and Troop were going to live there while he built a house for them."

"Well, I hope that Nora stays put in her house and doesn't wander into mine," said Grandmother Louise. "She can spend her first span of eternity accusing her new daughter-in-law of putting a crack in the good butter dish, and trying to hunt down where she's hidden her copper colander, and so forth."

"Why?" I asked. "Maureen sounds like a nice person."

"The woman sounds brilliant, but my household has earned the right to be selfish. You see, we all suffer when such a great lie as theirs is loose in the air. I can't tolerate having Troop be so full of, well, evil, about a man who is so enormously good. His father has to do something about pain, whether it is the misery of the living or the dead. And all these years he has had those two people accusing him of spoiling their lives by leaving them home from the party. But they weren't made to go anywhere, and the large social life stopped when she left. The woman was embarrassed by what little part of him she wasn't able to smother, and she demanded to leave. The way I see it, she was the very thing that drove him to take up with the nudists. No man in history has had such hell to pay for taking off his clothes."

Three

I was always told that ghosts heard about my grandparents' house, across the street from ours, on Dupont Circle through an odd grapevine, and after the telephone was installed, I began to think of the ghosts chatting on a party line, giving one another rendezvous instructions. Although Toby made the discovery that the house was haunted in 1876, the year he and Grandmother Leslie married and moved in, only when my father's parents moved in, twenty years later, did someone investigate further: Grandfather Leonard used his expertise in electromagnetism to detect that ghosts were actually attracted to the house and had converted it into a sort of rest stop for themselves. He took immediate charge of what had been chaotic. He stayed in the basement during the day, working out the complexities of his electromagnetic experiments, but at night he attended to the needs of the ghosts as though managing a house full of tired and unruly children. One night when Grandmother Leslie was kept up by what she called "the racket of the spheres," all of the ghosts expressing their aims and aggravations at once, she checked into the Willard, leaving a note that read: "Toby, if these lodgers knew how lucky they are that you waited until after Nora had left before you moved into this house they seem to admire so much, they would train themselves to be respectful and rest at night. She would have evicted them, barred the door, and gotten her beauty sleep."

Grandfather Leonard once told me that the recently dead invariably arrived at the house sadly baffled and that any person predisposed toward bewilderment should order his affairs and feelings early on in life, or arrange to avoid death altogether. When he intuited the presence of a new arrival, he reapplied his pomade, refreshened his shirt and collar, and sweetened his breath, as would any solicitous innkeeper. To comfort them and gain their trust, he asked them to tell him what in life had been their most earnest desire, and then he made them a gift of it, bearing in mind that he was mortal and thus enjoyed only limited capabilities. One could not say, for instance, "More than anything, I wished for my husband to be mauled by a pack of wild dogs," or "I longed to be the king of England." If a woman died by her own hand, she was asked what need had gone unmet so blatantly for so long that she chose this conclusion, and the need was met, for it was

usually achingly small and simple. Leonard once sat by the
dining room wall for half the night, singing "Old Folks at
Home" and dolefully squeezing his concertina to soothe a
drowned woman. He was always able to make a credible
claim of adoration to these lonely women, as he loved everyone who passed through those walls. He wanted the best
for them. If a man had died from the whiskey habit but was
parched nonetheless, he was told where the liquor was kept,
but then interrogated as to whether he truly wanted to stagger
and spew his way through eternity.

Leonard lined out the terms of the ghosts' leases and the
manner in which their individual infinities would be more
or less personally customized, reckoned by the choices they
had made while alive: "You will become the one thing that
brought you the most happiness. If it was the purity of love,
you're set. You will feel loved and be love itself at all times.
But if your chief pleasure was a chronic sadism wherein you
thrived on human misery and compounded it through your
own words and deeds, then you are not as set."

Because he had such an ethical heart, I did not have to hear
from the ghosts with my own ears to believe, when my
grandfather pulled a chair to the wall, placed his ear beside
it, and sat there for hours, that he was listening to what he
said was there. And all my grandparents were too pragmatic
and mindful of time to devote so much of it to something
that they had merely imagined into existence. When I was
sixteen, fear of being caught in the act of testing family loy-
alty kept me from marking the levels of liquor in the de-
canters after I was told that the ghosts were planning a party

for one among them who had poisoned herself on her birthday. But my brother, Daniel, who was fifteen at the time, had grown belligerent and intolerant of anything that was not normal in his life. He was especially frustrated that, although we were wealthy, although the money was there to buy him anything he wanted, it was not. He had been scouting for evidence that he could flag in his grandparents' faces to prove them fools or charlatans, but when he prosecuted them on the basis of the unchanged level of whiskey in the decanter, they said nothing and walked away. Later, he confronted them about a tray of unconsumed cream of tomato soup and rock-salt crackers—what an indigent boy ghost said he had unsuccessfully dreamed of being served all his nine years instead of his usual diet of boiled necks and moldy hardtack.

Our grandparents were vastly aggrieved by Daniel's menacing, yet said nothing; but Mother rebuked him each time he violated their privilege to live as they pleased. After the tomato soup confrontation, she sat him down. "The best things," she said, "are invisible, and invisible things are the only things safe to believe. Anything rooted in as much love and goodness as the care of these unsettled souls must be unequivocally believed. It is no different from when a Catholic says he is drinking the blood of Jesus Christ. He does not say it merely because the priest likes to hear that people have faith in something they can never touch. Which would you rather have at the end? Would you rather people remember you because of your fine clothes and your automobile or because you were an honorable and generous man? The wrong answer means I've failed you. It means I somehow created a monster. But you can learn better, and you will. And answer me this. Why are you so stubborn? We give you a good life. Why are you so determined against living it honestly and bravely?"

There would be many more lectures and disagreements before Daniel, who was gambling and drinking incessantly by the time he was sixteen, decided to run off to Baltimore with an older boy to work at a waterfront oyster saloon. Mother regarded his decision as just another episodic breach of common sense, and told her father, "He knows nothing about oysters and even less about doing a day's work. I would very much appreciate you going up there and dragging him home, and then I will make getting him sober and settled my around-the-clock occupation." But Daniel was back home within a week, after we received the news that he had been discovered dead on the floor of a hotel room. He had hanged himself. He was a large boy, and the chandelier and part of the ceiling, after a time, came down with him.

No doubt because of embarrassment over now participating in something he had so often doubted and damned, Daniel never passed through the walls of my grandparents' house the way my father had. Grandfather Leonard had come over and told Mother that her husband was asking for her. He found her sitting at the end of the kitchen table with her head in her hands, and said, "Grammar wants you to sit with him until the funeral starts." She smiled, took his hand, and walked out of the house.

When she came back, I went into her bedroom, where she had been sleeping in her clothes on top of the covers since my father's death. She was smoothing her stockings up her legs, and when I asked her what she had heard in the wall, she lifted her face and said, "Oh Mary, everything. Simply everything."

Although we might've saved the expense of running such a large house, Mother and I did not move in with my grandparents after my father and Daniel were gone, because she recognized how easy it would be for both of us to lose our independence. I sometimes thought of the street that ran between the two houses as the line that ensured that our identities remained individual and distinct. She made it clear that she welcomed their support, but the responsibility for raising me was hers. When I read, in a popular domestic-hygiene book, that children who were raised by hand, not by proxy, were more likely to contract nutritional-deficiency diseases like pellagra and rickets and were more prone to worms and head lice, I took such acute exception that for weeks I defiantly told anyone who asked anything remotely related to my home life that my mother raised me by hand. And I also felt the need to make sure people knew that even though we could afford squads of housekeepers and governesses, my mother's devotion to me made them unnecessary.

The Olivers and Greenes, combined, had among the largest family fortunes in Washington. And the inherited income from my father's estate was so huge that when Mother left his attorney's office and met me on the sidewalk, she was laughing so hard she had to catch her breath on a bench. When I was old enough to understand, she showed me the note my father had handwritten at the bottom of his will. "Martha, for God's sake," it read, "take some of this and hire someone to clean the house. I will love you forever, Grammar." He apparently had hoped that she would put an end to her famously nonchalant housekeeping, but she said, "I had rather leave the mess and take everybody to Europe for the summer. Wouldn't you?" Both households packed hurriedly, and sailed a week later, aware of the responsibility to help give Mother what she needed most, which was more time before she faced organizing the house and her life without him.

Regardless of the wealth, my grandparents still taught frugality as a virtue and a discipline. If I stayed with them on a school night, I was likely to be sent off the next day with a boiled sweet potato in a calico-covered bucket rather than with the potted meats and fancy tinned fruit cocktails that they were willing to purchase for me only if they could buy them in bulk on extreme markdown from the dented-goods rack at the decrepit surplus store they loved to rummage through. But they were all curious about modern intellectual and scientific advances, and would gather with others in large groups for long weekends on the Chautauqua circuit, hearing about psychoanalysis or quantum physics or socialism. Crates of books they bought on these trips were always unloaded and stacked on the train platform alongside their dilapidated luggage. When Daniel once argued that the family always seemed to have an abundance of money to spend on books about things people could not understand, Grandfather Leonard said, "Precisely. We pay to understand."

I knew we were blessed with a kind of general household intelligence, and it showed itself in the conversation that went on fairly much all the time. I associated the silence in the homes of some of the Sun and Moon Girls I visited with a poverty much more frightening than having no money to buy pretty things. Being poor, I believed, meant living in wordless gloom. I thought money bought conversation, and I was mortified that other families seemed to have run out or never to have had any at all.

My mother's way of arranging her generosity to look unplanned lightened the strain inherent between the two groups. When I was assigned to bring beverages to a Sun and Moon Girls trip to Rock Creek Park, she packed our copper samovar, because she thought it would be convenient for the girls to serve themselves, and she knew they would have fun using the elephant-trunk spout. That this unwieldy samovar had been lugged by pack animal and train, and smuggled out of Morocco in a case of fan knobs to avoid a luxury tax, made no difference to her, as long as the girls would like it. As I lay in my tent that night, I thanked the universe for keeping me free of want, squalor, filth, hookworm, pellagra, rickets, lice, and a family with nothing to say. And I was grateful for a mother who was willing to supply a samovar on an otherwise standard Saturday afternoon.

Neither the ghosts, the séances, the esoteric interests, nor the summer weekends my grandfather Toby spent at nudist camps destroyed the security of the family's established social position. This is what my uncle and his mother had so much difficulty understanding. We were always warmly welcomed at gatherings of Cavedwellers and Antiques, the old orders of Washington society, at embassy parties, at opening nights at the theater. We had never been subjected to a public shunning, nor had gossip reached us about being cut in private. Our record was not so different from that of families who count among their members a beloved morphine addict living in his old nursery or an adored deviant who is shackled to a chair and bolted into his room when nice ladies come over. We were never expected to change anything about our habits or ways to gain the favor of a more orthodox and normal society. It was as though there was a sign on the front door of my grandparents' home: "This is what we do. This is not a display or a fad. This is how we live. We appreciate your respect."

I didn't move away from them when I attended Goucher, and during the summers I spent at Radcliffe, at least one of my grandparents went with me. I graduated from Goucher in May of 1918 but was unable to return to Cambridge to complete the postgraduate work that was required before I began teaching a seminar there the next fall. So many people there, male and female, had been absorbed by the fighting and ancillary war work that there were not enough people left to either take or teach the literature classes. A lower-level course was available for me to teach in January of 1919, and I would have to wait for that.

But after seven months at home, I began to feel something close to resentment at being trapped. It wasn't just because of the practical matters of travel that everyone was having to adjust to; some insensible quality in the atmosphere made even the most independent and hardy spirits call for reassurance that everything was safe, that we were not going to be gassed on the trolleys or invaded, that we were not somehow accidentally going to lose the war. The need to know I would be fine pressed down on me like a coming storm. Sometimes after I read the morning paper, I would go find my mother wherever she was and would follow her around the house, close on her back, like a blind person following a sighted one.

It would have been disrespectful to complain about being housebound without then explaining to my grandparents that I intended to do something useful as soon as I finished reading my magazine or novel. I was repeatedly told that I would make a bully nurse, but I had no yearnings to take the expedited medical course that was being offered in church basements. And I had no desire to advance past the lowest ranks of the suffrage organization. Although I marched in parades, when one of the leaders learned that I had time available and asked whether she could put my name forward as an organizer, I thought of the hours Mother and I had spent debating with the mannish and combative women at their headquarters, and I declined.

My sense is that I crawled through the blistering Washington summer on my hands and knees. Early in September, when Mother saw me with a set of Russian-language books, she said, "I had no idea things were this acute. Learning Russian. I love you, Mary, and please don't be offended, but you have to find something to do. I've never felt like this. Being here with you has always been a pleasure, but I feel like you're tangling me in my own feet."

I told her that I certainly understood, that I would search the newspaper for any opportunity for temporary employment first thing the next morning. But I could not tell her that feeling compelled to pick up after her trail of strewn litter was beginning to grate on me. Perhaps we were simply discovering simultaneously that there eventually will come a time when a healthy and alert twenty-two-year-old woman needs to leave her mother's house. I was three or four days into collecting notices of employment from the newspaper when Mother sat down at the table with me and said, "You remember me telling you that Troop's wife is having a baby. I'm glad, because there's something so lonely about him. But you see, he sent a very nice note after he received my card. It came a few days ago, and I wanted to give myself a few days to think about it before I answered. I had written a little note with the anniversary card and mentioned that you were at home for the time being, and then when he responded, he mentioned that Maureen was due two or three weeks before Thanksgiving and also that he was traveling a great deal on business."

Already knowing the answer, I asked what all of this had to do with me. "Mary," she said, "he hasn't said anything ugly or unkind since the funeral, and when you get down there, if he's even unpleasant, you can turn around and leave, and we will never have anything to do with him again."

"Get down there?" I asked.

"Yes. Maureen needs something like a lady's companion for the duration, and you need something interesting to do until next term."

"Mother," I told her, "you've said he was evil incarnate, and now you want me to go stay in his house."

"I called him long-distance," she said. "I had to hear his voice before I made a decision. He was calm. He was peaceful. He sounded very proud to be having a baby. You know I wouldn't send you into anything unsafe or uncertain."

I asked when I was expected to leave, and what my grandparents had to say about this, especially about my being gone over the holidays.

"Tuesday, and nothing. I haven't told them yet. But you know we agreed after your father died that I wouldn't go trotting over there for advice about every decision that had to be made on your behalf, and this is one of those times when I did what I thought was best. Maureen is a beautiful woman. And now she's going to have a baby. You would be a world of help to a new mother facing Thanksgiving and Christmas. We'll celebrate again when you get back home. Just your presence will be a relief to her. You remember how I told you that I saw so much favor between you."

"Yes, Mother, that we were both open and trusting and would believe anything anybody told us."

"Yes, and believe me now. These next months of your life will always be a blessing."

Four

By Tuesday, my grandparents had adjusted themselves enough to the idea of my going to North Carolina to accompany Mother and me to Union Station. She had decided that no one would behave as though I were being sent off to my doom. But when we were on the platform, watching the line of people inch toward the steps of the southbound train, she said, "My God, if these individuals are any indication of the general population down there, maybe the South really *is* one big asylum." When I reminded her that Washington was southern, she smiled and said, "We've gone over that. It isn't."

Grandmother Leslie, recognizing that Washington's geographical status could be debated until people said they agreed with my mother, pushed the fashion magazines she had just bought down into my satchel and said, "Mary, I know none of us are snappy dressers, but this is the first time in my life that I've looked around Union Station and realized what an attractive group we are."

"You're exactly right," Mother said. "We never look this good when the train points in the other direction."

She watched an intoxicated woman board, and then a man with a grotesquely deformed head. "Mary, I think the time has come for you to move beyond what Daniel did," she said. "Let me run in there and exchange your ticket. You can go ahead and get your things moved up to where the first-class passengers are waiting."

I told her I was fine, and promised to buy a better ticket home in January, even though I had been promising to up-grade my accommodations for years. It seemed easier to ride fifteen hours in the middle of a rolling party than be trapped inside the memory of what I had come to think of as my brother's mortifying transportation demands. From the time he was old enough to be taken anywhere, he always insisted on superior amenities. He seemed to have been born with a fine-honed awareness of class distinctions. Even when we all went to Europe on the *Carpathia*, when I was nine and Daniel was eight, my father had to drag him out of his berth as he kicked and screamed that things weren't good enough. Father then made him sit on deck until he understood that go-ing overseas was blessing enough, and money was not going to be wasted so he could travel like a Vanderbilt. It was not a notion Daniel ever accepted, and we never went anywhere, from Maine to California, that he did not make both our parents' and then my mother's journey a demented and hellish experience. After his death in 1913, my family sailed to England on the *Lusitania* to spend the summer with some of Grandmother Leslie's relatives. Mother took one look at the vast, splendid scene and said, "I am so sorry to say this, but it would kill your brother all over again to know we're surrounded by this. I'm missing him for all the wrong reasons."

When we reached Devonshire, we found Grandmother's relatives were devout Luddites who, on a logic-defying level, invited hardships that my family would not have permitted in their lives for more than this summer. They lived without the simplest modern convenience, packed in a lean-to, cooking in a stone hearth and toting water from a creek. We settled into a nearby inn that featured narrow plank sleeping hammocks, raised off the floor on account of vermin, and a pond for washing clothes and bathing. Grandfather Toby sensed the presence of people in the area who might be friendly to the idea of nudism, and when he did find them, he would come back of an evening and swear he had been with Druids, although when he brought them to dinner once, they seemed more like aged, long-term alcoholics and dope fiends. Mother commented afterward that she had not counted ten teeth in anyone's head that entire summer in Northumberland, and then she smiled softly and said, "Daniel would have jumped into the ocean and swum home from here." What amazed me is that my grandparents were unfazed, both by the splendor on the *Lusitania* and the deprivation of the Luddite relatives.

When the nightly domestic disturbances at the inn had my mother and me in the hallways with the local constabulary, pointing out the revolving rounds of villains and victims, my grandparents saw it as free entertainment.

Daniel's ghost had never appeared in Washington, but my mother was incessantly surrounded by him on this trip. She suffered a plague of insomnia that was brought on by the memory of his scolding. One bleary-eyed morning she told me, "A mother never puts distance between herself and her child. Everything wounds. His grandparents weren't frightened of him because of the time and space between them. That's why they can sleep without having Daniel hound them."

She was right about Daniel's incapacity to injure his grandparents. They could stand before him, absorb a barrage of complaints and then walk away, saying, "We do not hear you." When Mother once asked whether it might be convenient for Daniel, who was eleven at the time, to be taken along when Grandfather Leonard attended a conference on hydroelectricity in Chicago, Grandfather told her, "Absolutely not. I would rather walk there and back."

My grandfather was recalling that Daniel, at the age of ten, caused an elderly family friend of modest means untold embarrassment when he visited her farm and demanded to leave early because he thought her circumstances too mean, her food too plain, and then at the train station he cried until he vomited because she could not afford to furnish him with a first-class ticket home. I knew that if I upgraded my ticket to Elm City, I would ride shoved in with the memory of my mother's fainting when she heard about the woman's turning her coin purse inside out in public, frantically searching for enough money to placate this *enfant terrible,* and feeling coerced into borrowing the difference in price from the station's attendant, which she evidently did do. Daniel arrived with an invoice from the attendant pinned to one of the shirts in his bag.

When the old woman came to Daniel's funeral, driven from her home in the automobile Mother sent for the two-hour trip, she hobbled in wearing an odd-fitting striped bustle skirt that she must have borrowed from someone who knew as little as she about what town ladies wear. It resembled a Vaudeville skating costume, but no one looked askance. Everybody knew the story of Daniel's extortion. Had he been able to speak from the coffin in our front parlor, there is no telling what appraisal he would've made of her finery. I remember thinking, without much contrition or even tact, Thank God we are all at last out of his range.

Sad to report, the only time Daniel rode by himself in something less than first class was when his body was brought back from Baltimore. But now, as I waited to board the train south, I could not think about him. After my mother and my grandparents had pulled me aside and secreted pocket money into my hands and made me promise to report any difficulties with Uncle Troop, to seek some outside company, to not spend all my free time with a book, and to let my uncle know right away that his father had torched his wardrobe and was now walking about downtown Washington naked, I left them, waving, watching.

We were all aboard—old, young, halt, hacking, and more than likely insane. Once the train was out of the tunnel, everything became active and loud in the sudden burst of light. I read the first chapter of *Anna Karenina* three times before I realized that I had no idea what the words said, and this reminded me of a professor who had told me that for one year she had lost her ability to read; "I went without my mind," she said. Everything in the compartment was distracting. The least of it was the intoxicated woman, who threatened to claw other passengers' eyes out if they did not stop staring at her. A young father terrified his daughter to the point of hysteria with a handful of Mexican jumping beans, and then she became locked in a long, chugging moan, what a deaf-mute might emit when trying, in vain, to indicate danger or need. A very thin boy came through the car, selling letters from Jesus Christ; he screamed and ran to his seat when the door at one end opened and in came the man with the unusual head whom my family and I had seen in line.

This man wasn't intentionally trying to terrorize us, but because of a series of congenital misfortunes, he simply could not help it. He was of indefinite age, as though he may have had an alert, youthful look about him until he walked out of his house one ordinary morning, wholly unawares, straight into seven years of sandstorms, locusts, floods, and droughts. He could very well have pressed a grisly and permanent impress upon children's nightmares. He had a warped, emaciated face, the jaw so deeply sunken that it might have been swallowed and then lodged in his throat. His startlingly wide and disproportionate cranium reminded me of textbook pictures of inmates whose heads were measured with the Bertillon system and who were diagnosed as organically demented or libidinously degenerate, and summed up in captions such as: "Bank Robber—Mental Defect—Murderer—Needs Hanging." The man was with me for the length of the journey, walking slowly from one end of the train to the other. I heard him speak only twice.

Occasionally I was assaulted with strong, purgatorial waves of something that had the same unmistakable odor of the rotting, composted vegetable matter my grandparents used for fertilizing their kitchen garden. When I reached underneath my seat to look for a book in my satchel, I noticed the man beside me removing his elderly mother's shoes. He was thinking out loud, contriving the source of money to purchase the rolling chair he had promised her. She became highly disconcerted and seemed to be struggling to kick him in the face. He peeled off the several pairs of thin, pilled wool stockings she had secured at her knees with mismatched ribbon, rolled them into a wad, and pushed them and her cheaply cobbled Congress shoes beneath his seat. Her feet seemed to have lost their quick. They were hardened, ill-formed, knotted, and variously colored, as though she had soaked them in Mercurochrome and then rinsed them with bluing.

Her son tried to calm her. He was telling her that Sears, Roebuck had let her down on her shoes, when the deformed man returned. He stopped in the aisle and looked down at her feet, then spoke.

"Excuse me, but I have to ask: Are those feet real or something they stuck on the end of your legs when you lost yours? Because if they are real, and it was me, I'd hack them off at the ankles."

He turned around and asked whether I did not agree.

I said, "I'm sorry, but I don't have an opinion."

The son started to speak, but his mother said she was capable of answering this fool. And then she snarled, "Are you a doctor? If you are, bring on the hatchet. If not, toddle on."

Another woman upbraided her, saying, "Leave him be. He's probably a veteran and had something blow up in his face."

"Then if he is a veteran," the shoeless woman answered, "he ought to behave."

A general discussion about veterans and the characteristic injuries of different wars developed, and it was agreed that the current barbarism of gas and trenches was a fair indication that the next war would be fought in hell. There were no soldiers who could be consulted in the compartment, as they were all riding together in the back of the train, but the only silent miles that were to be had along that journey came after a woman said, "They buried my son at Belleau Wood. You know nothing about it. Hush and be still."

Five

M ost of the Great War casualties were coming back
with great damage to their faces and upper torsos, the
first parts of themselves available to be destroyed when they
came up over the top of the trenches. I had seen only a few
of those who had recuperated enough to be out in the world
again. Although the deformed man was not as young as the
others who had been in France, his scars said he had suffered
horribly there. But when we disembarked in Elm City, I
overheard him tell several veterans who greeted him like one
of their own, "Thank you, but it was a pint of carbolic acid
chunked at me in 1888." He invited them to enjoy a glass of
steam beer with him, but they said they had to make a living,

although they did appreciate the invitation. They were pushing trunks and carrying bags for passengers, and some of them could not manage. The more able men stepped forward and helped, wordlessly, then picked through the change in their palms and made sure the tips were split correctly. While I was waiting for Zollie, the Ross household's "useful man," to collect me, I noticed two wild-eyed and despairing boys barely staying upright on a bench beside the station, shocked, blistered, and muttering, aged into very old men by the mustard gas that must have fallen on them like rain in Flanders.

Tall and thin, with hair that was going to gray at the temples, Zollie appeared to be between thirty-five and forty. He was gotten up like the headwaiter at the Ritz, and before we left the station he reached behind his seat and exchanged his hat for a sporty khaki driving cap to wear on the mile-or-so ride home. He said that his wife, Mamie, the housekeeper, had covered a plate for me before she went home to tend to their two children, eight-year-old twin boys named Turner and Wells.

"I didn't intend to put anyone out," I told him. "I should've asked my uncle to come and get me."

"No," he said. "Mr. Ross goes to bed at nine o'clock. It isn't any kind of problem. But Mrs. Ross certainly wanted to see you tonight."

He said that he would make sure I was settled, then be back at five, and that he was willing to pick up any special breakfast requests before I awakened. I wondered how anyone could be so nonchalant about this continued enslavement, which he seemed to be passing off as dedication to his employer.

When he told me we were driving down the Rosses' street, I replied that, even in the dark and mist, I could see it would be a lovely place to stroll a new baby. He said quietly, "If God is merciful, yes. But everything is in its own time."

This indicated to me that the family was committed to the old tradition of keeping the household free of any sign of the coming birth, whether it be pretty baby things or conversation about the event. Even people with habitual access to sophisticated medical care still would not dare do anything toward preparing the home to receive a child, a superstition certainly, yet one grounded in sad truth. Babies popped up in families and startled siblings. Expectant mothers draped and swooped on extra layers of chiffon and silk, and never let on. The cause was usually laid to fear of bad luck, but in truth it was their acceptance of probability and their acknowledgment that everyone in the home need not be wrenched up into a frenzy of hope that might be dashed to ruination by a house full of grief: Here comes another baby, more joy all around—and then a fever, pertussis, diphtheria, rubella, any of the other many claimants to the souls of mothers and their infants. In those days even the plumpest and loudest and rudest infants were not fully, justifiably celebrated until true promise of life was assured, when they were at least three months old.

The Ross house was situated on a corner, at the top of sloping grounds. Even in the dark, it was imposing. Our house on Dupont Circle was rickety in comparison to this massive stone affair. I entered an oval foyer that was plastered a chalky white and thickly carved, like a wedding cake or a sugar-spun Easter egg. I had expected the entry to be dark, in keeping with the outside of the house, but as I followed Zollie through the downstairs and up the wide curving staircase to Maureen's room, I realized that there was no continuity; I was more or less hit in the face with varying, grand visions. It was as if someone had decided what impressive scene should be presented next, and then set about accumulating the most magnificently expensive and overwrought merchandise they could find to put in room after room.

Not more than two or three days before I left Washington, the chair Grandmother Louise was sitting in at dinner cracked and tipped her out onto the floor, for no apparent reason. While we were helping her up, she declared herself furious at her father for not having fixed the chair correctly in 1857, when it broke the first time, and she broke her elbow. Most of the interiors of the houses in our neighborhood looked to have been similarly long worn, the furnishings passed down, impacted with beeswax. Unless one's house had caught fire, buying a new piece of furniture required justification and was generally considered evidence of climbing. As I walked through rooms that were done to the point that they could not have taken another tassel or trinket without having the entire conglomeration collapse under its own weight, I sensed something adamant, almost pathetic, and what caused the greatest unease was the intimation that everything was packed with family history, but not of the family inhabiting those rooms. A coat of arms was placed conspicuously on the wall near the foot of the stairs, and I wondered whether it had been purchased at some point in the family's history, along with the name, the way people buy the name of a ruined aristocrat and outfit themselves with a lineage, like D'Urberville.

Standing there after midnight in a hallway lined by store-bought portraits of ancestors, I felt nothing but contempt for my uncle and his mother. I had learned that Nora's family wealth came from the creative and lucrative convict-leasing scheme that her grandfather established the day after slavery was abolished. That money bought her way into Elm City society, such as it was, and into a woman's college in northern Virginia, where she met my grandfather at a party on the James River. I wanted to ask Zollie, who was putting my things in a bedroom before he took me to meet Maureen, "Who are all of these people on the walls?" I featured in my mind the piteous image of a boy and his mother at a Saturday-morning flea market, picking through the bins of castoffs and unsold leavings from estate sales, searching out the most distinguished lot of ladies and gentlemen who might be said to bear some family favor.

Maureen's room was at one end of the hall, and my uncle's was at the other. Both had double doors, with heavily carved molding around them and stained-glass transoms above. Zollie indicated that I was to go meet Maureen by myself. Pointing to the far right of her dimly lit room, he whispered, "She stays over there."

I walked through the room, past a canopied bed with a silver satin–covered bench at the foot. Although I could not make out any details, I could see enough to know that they were unique in relation to what I had seen of the rest of the house. Instead of the William Morris wallpaper that changed pattern from room to room downstairs, her walls were a faint ocean blue. Every surface that could held vases of roses, of every color and variety conceivable. I heard her call my name, and I followed her voice around a corner into a small alcove surrounded by tall Florida windows, which were cranked wide open despite the wet mist outside. She turned up the lamp beside the purple velvet chaise she lay on, and spoke carefully and quietly. "I like to let the weather in and clean up later. How are you, Mary? Did you travel well?"

The fatigue from all those hours on the train, the petulance over the unnecessary servitude and the fraudulent ancestors in the hall, any other strain and anxiety, vanished. Maureen was sheer wonder, layered in ivory silk, her thick black hair upswept and tied with a long black grosgrain ribbon. She lay on her side, with her long legs bent at the knees and her arms underneath her stomach, supporting the weight of the baby. After she got herself standing and hugged me, instead of going on to bed, she lay back down on the chaise and pulled the quilted green blanket over her hips and legs, telling me, "This chaise is better than a board on my back. I can get in bed again in fifty days."

When I asked if she needed anything before bed, she only reminded me that supper was waiting if I wanted it. I should sleep late in the morning, as she doubted she would need me then, either. And then, lowering the light by the chaise, she said, "In fact, you can go and do as you please. We have a new moving picture theater here. If I think of something I need, I can send Mamie. But I thank you for coming, even if it is under false pretenses."

"False pretenses?" I asked.

"I'm sorry," she said, "but I hardly need a social secretary. Maybe the company would be nice, though, somebody to be in a nice mood. How long are you going to stay?"

"Until January." I was surprised that she didn't know.

"Oh, well then, good night, and thank you," she whispered, and closed her eyes.

I settled in that first night, thinking how her sweetly baffled affect was so like the manner common among ancient former slaves I had met as a child in Washington, the women who sold baskets and flowers near the fountain at Union Station. They had withstood decades of hurt but were then blessed by heaven with a thorough, absentminded forgetfulness. When Maureen's distraction was just as apparent the next day, I wondered whether something horrible had happened just before my arrival.

It was almost hypnotic to watch her as she ranged about her room in a state of heightened unreality, as though that was the perfect and only place she could find true consolation. She would stop, turn her face to a wall, and weep, saying, "Excuse me, please," when I tried to help. I had been with Mamie in the kitchen early that morning, but she had not mentioned any sudden shock, such as a bad report from the doctor, and when I found her again and asked her outright what was happening in the house that I should know about, anything that would help me help my aunt, Mamie said, "Nothing out of the ordinary that I know of. Zollie and I keep an eye on her."

"What can I do?" I asked.

"Lay her back down," Mamie said, "and let her rest. Mr. Ross comes home at the regular time tonight, and she needs to be up for that."

"She wouldn't want to go out for a short walk?"

"Not today. I would leave it be."

Maureen slept most of that day, and when she was awake, she was unable to engage herself in anything but worry that I was going to be angry with her for wasting my time. She slept in this beautiful space she had created for herself, with the pale blue and green, the deep violet and lavender, the brown and iridescent silver, that told me she had been alert enough to figure this out when she moved here. My impression, when the full morning light came in through those tall windows on that first day I was in the house, was that she had somehow improved on nature. The colors in her room could all be seen when I looked outside, but hers were better.

On the table beside her was a collection of Edna Ferber's short stories, but the pages were uncut, and there wasn't a paper knife around anywhere, unless it was under the heaps of fallen rose petals. I thought I might glance at it while she napped, so I opened a cabinet to hunt for a knife, and inside I saw fifty or so books stacked haphazardly, nothing light or trivial. Tucked into the back of the cabinet, where I also finally found the knife, was a stash of pocket travel guides to everywhere a person might possibly go if she did not weep at the prospect of going outside. I thought of the times that Maureen had been mentioned in her husband's notes over the past few years and realized that he had evidently forgotten to mention some things about her basic nature. "Maureen is thriving." "Maureen appreciates the shawl you sent. She loves to wear it when she goes about." "Maureen's friends all envy the hair combs you last sent."

Mother believed that Maureen had never written a line herself. But she did send tasteful, appropriate gifts on holidays and birthdays, things ordered from better department stores, which managed to feel personally selected nonetheless. Now that I saw her, I also saw how ridiculous it was to think of her perched on the edge of one of those gilt chairs in the downstairs parlor, writing a bread-and-butter note. That she had been able to send us the orchid pots, the pewter chafing dish, the scrimshaw hair ornaments, and the silk brocade wrappers now seemed miraculous. Mother was always sure these gifts had been chosen by a woman. "Nothing about them," she said, "is ever off." The first gift she had sent to us after Nora's funeral was Edith Wharton's decorating book. Mother and I were both amazed, as we loved her novels, but we had not known of this fascinating book. Mother sat down and read it like a novel, saying again and again that she could not imagine such unprovoked thoughtfulness from this woman she barely knew. I had to wonder whether Maureen had been such a shadowy figure in the background because of a natural reticence or an unnatural restraint.

And now I was watching this thoughtful, expectant woman

open her eyes straight into mine, frantic, saying, "Oh God, it's almost dark out. I have to go thank him now. I must go thank him. Please help me get up."

Among the few words she said all day were, "Thank you, but Troop dislikes my room, so I keep the door closed. He says my room ruins the house." She hurriedly pulled herself together and spent the next few minutes practicing tones of voice with which she would greet her husband when he entered the house promptly at seven-thirty and thank him for the roses that had arrived earlier in the day. I followed her downstairs to the foyer and listened to her rehearse, repeating to herself in varying earnest tones and volumes until she thought she had it the way he wanted to hear it. "Troop, thank you so much. Thank you. I want to thank you for the flowers, and I am so very glad for you to be home. And Mary, please tell him how happy you've been today and how I've seen to it that you have everything you need."

"I have, but is this necessary?" I asked her.

"Oh God, yes. How does it sound to you?"

"Aunt Maureen, I do not know you at all, but I think you would need to be a professional actress to do something like this."

She sighed. "I wish you hadn't said that. Now I have to start all over. But please call me Maureen."

She held her very large stomach and eased her body down onto a step. And then she started rehearsing again. "Just be ready to haul me up off the steps," she said, "when I'm ready to stand."

Mamie, without her apron, joined us in the foyer just before my uncle was due to arrive, as she did each day, no matter, she said, "if I am up to my elbows in lard."

Even in walking weather, Zollie drove Uncle Troop the ten blocks home from his office at the Duke brothers' tobacco concern, but Zollie could not come through the main door. He let Troop out at the walkway and then began his own routine. He parked the automobile, wiped it down with a fresh chamois cloth, and hung his duster in the garage. Then he came in the house through the kitchen, took his valet jacket from a hook in the pantry, and walked swiftly to my uncle's bedroom, where he brushed and laid out his evening clothes. He would brush each piece again in my uncle's presence, and then brush again once the clothing was on my uncle's body.

To my mind, only the great houses in places like Newport had carried this degree of formality over from the last century—daily life that does not admit muddy shoes or curtains unevenly drawn, with everything stylishly arranged, as though staged for an elaborate tableau vivant, and people in formal dress, sitting on the edges of their seats with their hands in their laps. And then the stillness sometimes made me feel as though we were all perpetually waiting for a body to be brought down.

He entered the house with a quiet sort of aplomb. He wanted me to say how happy I was to meet him and that I had everything I needed, and I did. The way he breezed in, so oblivious of the gloom already in the air and the extra dread he was bringing in with him, I understood my aunt's rehearsal, and so I heard myself speaking with her same apprehension.

He gave me his coat and said, "Careful." I wanted to scream, "I am not your servant, I am not your poor relation," but I only held the coat, as carefully as one can hold a wool overcoat, and waited until somebody could tell me what to do with it.

My uncle was a man of superb figure. If he had had additional size, it would have been too much, as overwrought as the house. He still took up a great deal of space in the room, and he knew it, using this awareness to his advantage, to make us all back up and give him more. As he turned to Maureen, the strain in the house increased to the level that people must feel when they are locked on the inside of a seizure. I had attributed any nervousness about meeting him to everything I had heard and read, but now that I was beside him, I remembered my mother's description of how she had bested him after the funeral, and I could not imagine how she'd managed it. I already felt threatened by how he smiled and inquired after my comfort.

"Have you let your mother know you arrived safely?" he asked.

"Yes," I told him. "I wrote."

And then, remarkably, he asked, "What did you say?"

"That everything was fine," I answered.

Maybe I was to say that I had told my mother that I was so happily settled in this beautiful place that I could not ever see myself returning home to our neighboring shacks full of crazy people. Maybe I was to say, "I notified her that you have obviously won, and everyone should go ahead and start eating themselves alive with envy."

He turned to Maureen, who touched his arm before she spoke. "Troop," she said, "you should not have sent the roses today. You do too much for me already. But I do thank you. You know how much I love Lady Hillingdon. And the card was very sweet."

She was a terrible actress. For all the rehearsal, she was tentative and edgy. He removed her hand from his sleeve, as if picking off a piece of lint. And then he went upstairs, saying nothing but nonetheless looking disappointed in the careless lack of trying on her part.

Sitting down on a carved gilt chair, she said, "I'm too heavy to be on this, but I have to stay here and blow a while before I go back up there. Mary, I don't mean to treat you like a day-wage slave, but if you could bring supper up for us, I would appreciate it."

"The two of you are not going to eat together now?" I asked.

"Oh, no," she said, "just you and me. He can talk to me later. Maybe you could stick your head in his room and tell him that my legs have swollen, and then I need to sleep. And one more thing. I think you want to go home now, don't you, Mary? I would if I were you."

"No, I don't want to go home, not right at this instant," I told her. "But this is quite a situation, and I just want to know what I've walked into. I should know what kind of what my family calls uproar and onslaught we may be in for with this child on the way."

She reached out her arm for me to lift her. "If I knew, I'd tell you. But for the life of me, I do not know."

"Maureen," I asked suddenly, "is your mother coming when you deliver?"

"No," she said, without lifting her head.

"Has she been to visit here?"

"No."

"Maureen, is your mother well enough to come at Thanksgiving?"

"I don't know. I write her every week, but I think she may be angry with me for something. I never hear anything. I told her about the baby, and still, nothing. It's as though everybody in Mississippi has died."

Six

The greeting ritual repeated itself until I took my uncle aside and told him that his wife had no business going up and down the stairs in her condition. I knew absolutely nothing about medicine and even less about symptoms of an impending stroke, but it sounded authentic enough to say that she was due for one if she did not stay recumbent as much as possible. Not until later did it occur to me how natural it would've been for him to call her doctor, but he said only, "Fine. No one requires her to trot downstairs when I get home. She calls these things upon herself and taxes the entire household."

But as was happening all that first week, I was hearing his

version of the story, delivered with purpose and authority, while hers was typically told through tears. Mamie and Zollie seemed direct enough when their employer was away, and then maddeningly timid in his presence. They could see the truth, but their position and race made any defiance or rebuttal impossible. The household had never been visited by anyone who either stayed long enough or moved far enough into the interior to see what was true and what was merely another pretty scene, orchestrated for public viewing, but I kept telling myself, "You are here now." People saw the roses go into the house, and that was all. They did not know the degree of gratitude owed Troop Ross for that day's delivery, and that there was to be no whiff of reproach for whatever he had said or done the night before that brought on the regretful necessity of another dozen.

Maureen was also supposed to mention the tastefully worded cards that were always attached so as to eliminate any question of his tender remorse and innermost sorrow. But because of the florist's mistaken use of a black-bordered card for several of the deliveries, people without intimate knowledge of that home assumed they were the funerary tributes of an eloquent second cousin. I thought it must periodically slip my uncle's mind that his wife had not been ordained with the same command over life and death that he and all men of such momentous influence enjoyed, for there was also sometimes this postscript on the cards: "Maureen, do not allow these flowers to die." I found dozens of the cards scattered in the bottoms of her drawers. One of the first things I did on her behalf was to gather and burn them while she was sleeping.

She was supposed to thank him as though the flowers were merely an excited utterance of his affection. Nothing in her voice could say, "Thank you for another deceitful substitution for true emotion. I wish these roses meant that you will never ridicule me again, that you will never say that I belong in Mississippi with the rest of the oafs or that our neighbors secretly find me common, and, for certain, that you will never hurt me again and send me more of these meaningless flowers. And then I would not have to worry about those neighbors who see them being delivered, who think, What a beloved woman Maureen Carlton Ross is, and how fortunate she is to be married to a man who showers her with roses and overlooks her heinous flaws."

He could not have chosen a more appropriate symbol than the rose to stand for the patina of life in that household. I wondered whether he had not chosen that flower specifically because no woman in her right mind would make any complaint against roses. If he had chosen orchids, then she could have gently complained that the orchid is a mean and stubborn variety and that to make it thrive requires expert understanding or a knack. She could have safely declared herself to have neither, and they could have been removed. But to argue against cut roses would be ungracious, and he would deftly manipulate his words so that she would feel mortified for having opened her mouth.

One would not generally hold that manipulation is accept-

able in a marriage, no matter how aggrieved the woman be-
lieves herself to be, but my uncle's behavior went far beyond
calling for his wife to be routinely mendacious as a means of
keeping the peace. His conduct celebrated the deceit and
cheered the lies along. Traps, deep holes for the unalert, lay
everywhere. I could not make out a true and thoughtful line
in the structure, which was more than enough reason for me
to wonder when the foundation would collapse on itself. I
learned that before she was expectant, if she feigned physical
illness, the daily criticisms and exacting reprisals would
cease, though only until he decided that she'd been sick long
enough. She trusted the lie to give her a reasonable expectation of serentiy. Once she became pregnant, things improved
for a while.

"I felt as though I was at a resort," she told me. "He was
kind and attentive, like at the beginning. But when the nausea and the fatigue of carrying the baby started, he told me
that women had babies all the time and that I was highlight-
ing things for attention. That was that. It was my fault. I
shouldn't have cried wolf so much back then."

When she told me this, she was lying on her side on the
purple chaise, where, it seems, she had spent most of the last
few years perfecting the art of taking responsibility for her
own misery. I asked whether she realized that it was not normal for any woman to be isolated in her own house and de-
pendent on what attention her husband chooses to dole out.

And that is when she said she had not been honest with
me, but had been afraid that if I had known she suffered from
"female hysteria," I would've walked out. I had been there

two weeks and seen nothing to indicate violent swings of mood, hysteria, nothing but loneliness and confusion. I had to ask, "Maureen, with things the way they are, why did you decide to have a baby?"

"Oh, I know that," she said, brightly and eagerly, as though excited to hear a question she could easily answer. "The last time I went for treatments, they said I needed a hysterectomy, and Troop agreed that I could have a baby first."

I was stunned. "Did you do anything to make him think something so drastic was necessary?"

"I can't say if there was one thing. More like an accumulation of things that made his skin crawl."

"And they were what?"

"The way I talked and ate. The way I wanted my own way with more of this house than just my room. The way I was nervous around his friends. The doctors he hired tried everything, but nothing changed. You don't want to hear all of this."

"Maureen," I said, "this is your home. Women get a say in how their homes look."

"Maybe, if you're Alice and Alva Vanderbilt and know something."

"Look at this room," I said. "I tried to describe the bedroom and sitting area to my mother, and couldn't."

"You could've told her that they're too odd. He threatened to bring the doctor in here and show him what I had done."

"Then I must be hysterical," I said.

"No, you're not. I met your mother. She wasn't crazy. You would have gotten it from her."

"My mother," I said, "came back to Washington and told us all how beautiful and smart and kind you were."

"Maybe I was, back then. Troop liked me so much, but people like me get tedious. I look back and see myself carrying on after my sisters died, and it's mortifying. They died four years ago, in a house fire in Yazoo City. We had been married only a little over a year, and I set up a wail to go to Mississippi. There wasn't and still isn't anywhere for him to stay there, so he couldn't go. But I wouldn't stop addling him to go."

"Maureen," I said, "people call that grief."

"I'm sure it was, but he barely knew them, my sisters Ella and Eloise. He hardly needed to listen to me day in and day out. It interfered with everybody's happiness. I went for a treatment that he put a great deal of faith in—it worked about a week and stopped. You see, I didn't start out the marriage being critical of him, but then I set up complaints about how nervous I was because of the loads of money being poured into this house. I asked about the possibility of some of it being sent to Mississippi. He pointed out how my family would waste it. And then he found a check I was going to send to fix Mama's house after a flood. He wanted me to stop making my own dress patterns also. It was humiliating for him to have to take me places and have me wear something I'd run up at home. He was right.

"He says he should have left back then, that he's felt swindled. He says he was promised a contented wife, but then he was saddled with a melancholic nag. But after the hysterectomy, I'll be the person who I promised to be. He won't have to regret me anymore. It's that simple. One doctor said that my womb was wandering around my body, sucking up energy and good sense, like a sponge. He tried for several weeks to massage it back into place. He even gave me my own vibrating belt so I could do my own therapy between appointments, but Troop threw it away and found another doctor, who believed surgery was the only answer. These other treatments have been drawn out over time, and very difficult for him."

"For him? What was done to him?"

"He had to have his hopes dashed every time something failed." She described how hard it had been on her husband for her to be shoved naked into a tub of ice, tranquilized into a stupor, beaten with wet towels, spun at a high velocity in the "Rotary Chair," subjected to vaginal fumigation, and hitched to a galvanic battery and shocked back into a more permissible sensibility.

"You do hear yourself when you say this, right? These things were done to your body, yours, not anyone else's. And I may be fresh out of college, but I don't believe you need such an important part of you carved out because a man doesn't like your opinions. We're not talking about your tonsils. I wish you could have heard my mother describing the dress you wore at the funeral, describing everything about you. And she's a hard woman to impress. About the money spent here, as opposed to sending some to Mississippi, you had every right to sling the nastiest tantrum he'd ever seen. If that had happened in my house, any one of the three women up there would've thrown everything in the front yard, set fire to it, and charged people to watch it burn. And then they would've taken up a collection on top of that and sent it wherever they pleased."

"That's because your family has money. Troop's mother was about to starve. He had to work an unbelievable amount to pay her expenses and ours. That's why he was so insulted that I wanted to take some of his money and send it to people who he says have no conception of what it takes to rise in the world."

"Maureen," I said, "do I seem like an honest person to you?"

"Yes, but I'm not the best judge of character. You'll see how many friends I have. I tend to pick fair-weather people."

"Well, this is the truth. Your husband has more money than God. His mother did. And then, my family sent an enormous amount over the years. Let me ask you: Why did your husband wait till his mother was dead before he brought you to see her?"

"Because he didn't want to upset her and make her think he loved somebody more than her."

"Has that ever seemed strange to you?"

"Yes, and so I waited until after we were married and settled to bring it up. I thought I was being respectful. He said it was anything but."

"I imagine he did."

"The stress, you see, that I caused by pulling him away when he needed to be with her those last two years is what caused her to go downhill and then die." She closed her eyes and would say nothing else.

She slept for a few hours, and when she awakened, she panicked until she located her "book." I thought she was keeping some diary or list about the baby. My mother had told me that women customarily start to feel a need to get everything in order and tie up loose ends, and since nothing was being purchased and set aside, she was probably writing down what she would need brought into the house after the delivery. Instead, she was recording the varieties of the roses Troop sent, studying and working at the list in a small volume of unlined blue parchment paper given to her for that purpose. It was best for her that she show specific indebtedness, which moved this broad-daylight larceny of her free will far across the line one could draw between the peculiar and the obsessive. These were hauled in soon after my arrival: Beauty of Rosemawr, Dr. Grill, Étoile de Lyon, Marie d'Orléans, Duchesse de Brabant, Homère, Mrs. Dudley Cross, and Rubens. I wasn't allowed to record them for her. She had to do it. It had to be done. He would check the book now and then to make sure everything was written in her hand.

Soon I was writing home, telling my mother that I felt safe, that I would be fine, that I was going to stay and take care of Maureen, despite the fact that nothing was as it had seemed to us and that underneath the surface of benign respectability was something hard and ugly. Nothing about her half brother had changed, I told Mother:

> Today, I learned that the state motto here is "To be rather than to seem." I think they forgot to inform Troop. I know

that since his mother's death he stopped demanding money, but it certainly does not appear to be needed. It seems that the only honest thing he told you in five years is that he moved his bride into a showplace. Otherwise, Mother, he created a world of false impressions for you, but I hardly see him admitting that he's still a vicious fraud, and his lovely wife has become a despairing but determined recluse.

I know you remember that story, "The Yellow Wall-Paper," the one Charlotte Perkins Gilman wrote about a woman's descent into madness after her husband, the physician, strips her of everything that is dear to her and then shuts her in the nursery. Remember how she strips the wallpaper, fighting to get out? Mother, I feel as though I have found a door that opens into this story, and let me tell you that despite the fact that Maureen does not have yellow wallpaper, there is no meaningful difference between the two worlds, the imagined one and this real one.

On the way down here, I was congratulating myself on being a perfect person, about to walk into a near-perfect set of circumstances, make some minor adjustments, and then leave them forever thinking, "What a perfect young woman Mary was. We were so fortunate to have her in our lives." But instead I am with a woman who needs something far beyond my encouraging her to cheer up and look on the bright side. The problem is that I have never been around anything like this, and having read of it in novels is useless. She has been subjected to all the "treatments" you and I were reading about when I left, and let me tell

you that she is not exactly a testimonial to their effective-
ness. She is convinced that she needs a hysterectomy to
make her more pleasant to be with, but I find her more
than pleasant. Sad, certainly, but absolutely wonderful.

I think that he despises her, though I cannot say why,
other than that he needs to beat back what is good and
worthy in her so that he can be superior in all things. Re-
member the way he blamed you all for his mother's death?
He also blames her, or tells her that he does. I'm sure he
doesn't believe it, and has said it only to wound. Please do
not be shocked. He has been rather quiet around me, but I
wonder if he does not think I'm plotting to undermine
him. If I were as perfect as I thought I was when you
arranged this enterprise, I would know all the answers.
But I don't blame you. It wasn't as though you were too
eagerly trusting. The man is very good, violently good
at what he does.

I was sitting by Maureen, reading with her, when my uncle
came in without knocking and said, "I've been expecting
you to bring me the blue book."

"She hasn't been well," I told him.

"Thank you, Mary, but Maureen knows what to do. This
doesn't concern you." Looking around the room, he said,
"You could help Maureen not let these flowers go."

"Well, they do tend to die."

"Replacements are certainly sent with enough frequency,"
he snapped.

"Uncle Troop," I said, changing the subject, "this isn't any of my business, but do you think we could perhaps keep some fruit up here, not for me, but because of the baby?"

"If I said yes, how do I know she would eat it? Would you, Maureen? Or would it stay up here and draw pests?"

I had needed to show her how unreasonable he could be about something she needed, something that should've been given without argument or challenge. She glanced at me and then said to him, "Yes, I'd eat it. I'd love some fresh fruit. Can I tell Mamie to buy some?"

"She can buy it, but it will be brought up here by the piece, and the refuse taken straight down. This house isn't going to be destroyed by vermin. Now, I came in here for the book."

It had slipped under the chaise. The few seconds it took Maureen to locate it were more than he could manage. He told me to go downstairs. I left the room and stood in the hall. Whispering and weeping were all I heard until he said, "You will use a pleasant tone of voice when you speak to me. You will do it."

I opened the door and went back in. He brushed by me as I passed the bed. He looked straight ahead, infuriated, running his hands through his hair repeatedly. She was weeping. She said, "He said I needed to lower my voice. I don't know what that means anymore."

I told her that she had not raised her voice, that I had heard.

"You did?" She seemed genuinely to need to know, not just to need reassurance.

"Yes," I told her. "You rest now. I'll stay."

From the beginning, I felt the need to be physically close to her. She endured her husband's bruising neglect, and if his conscience, the most intimate authority he had, could not convert him, neither could I. But I could offer her what he withheld, and given her grace, loving her was effortless.

"I love having you here," she said. "There's room beside me. I didn't know what it felt like to have an entire bed to myself until I got married."

I lay beside her, thinking that if I could be nothing else to her except another set of eyes and ears, that was better than nothing, more than what she had. I saw that when he confronted her, it was so close upon her and so evenly spoken that someone observing the two of them from across the room might later testify that Troop's obvious expressions of intimacy to his wife did not warrant her disproportionate, weepy reaction. And I probably would have been one of them had I not been listening to the exchange about the blue book, the fruit, and a dozen other trivialities during those early weeks.

If she had looked at me as someone who was now in the house who might believe her complaints, besides the stereotypically unreliable colored maid, and effect some kind of escape, and had I not known the substance of his words and his history with my family, I would have listened patiently and dismissed her. I would've gone directly to him and expressed myself, no doubt saying, "I hope I'm not betraying any confidence or overstepping my bounds, but your wife told me that you've been whispering things to her and saying she's responsible for your mother's decline, and you took issue with her sending money to her mother after a flood. I'm sure it's the expectancy that's made her so far disordered in the mind." He would not have corrected me.

When I had been there about a week, four ladies appeared with small gifts to welcome me to Elm City. They had heard Maureen was unwell, and wondered what they might do, while silently they prayed I would say, "Thank you, but she doesn't need a thing." They seemed to be the type of ladies who were honestly busy with their own lives, and finding the time for this visit was as far as mercy would take them. They definitely did not want to be pulled down into a morass. And because my uncle had so often ignored the rule of etiquette that prohibits a husband from speaking ill of his wife's behavior, no matter how scandalous, he had given them enough information to be able to assume the rest and conclude that Maureen Ross was lucky not to be facing long-term commitment to the asylum for nervous women in Plymouth, and that, moreover, she was lucky to still be married.

And when they asked, "Is there anything we can do for her? We can sympathize with these last weeks before the baby," I thanked them and said she didn't need a thing.

"Well, I know Troop's glad to have you here," one of them said. "And it's not only wonderful that he has someone young and bright to help him manage, it's good for you to have a nice place to stay for a while also."

I assumed they had heard I was the poor relation, that I'd been living inside a tree stump or a pasteboard box at Rock Creek Park and had come down from Washington out of desperation. I said nothing. There was not anything I could do but smile and nudge them toward leaving. There was no way of saying, "He tells it as he wants it told. He shows what he wants shown. Actually, you know nothing."

In the main, he wanted a wife who would see him through the eyes of these polite acquaintances. She couldn't do this, because she was married to him and had assumed all grades of intimacies that he now repelled. And neither could his servants escape the roiling stress that was part of living there. They were wordless around him, giving the sense of having long before traded their right to express an opinion about a brand of soap openly in front of him for the right to work for him and support their children. Lying on Maureen's behalf, when they were certain they would not be caught, was their principal means of protecting her. If they were caught, as when Maureen asked Mamie to bring an entire bowl of fruit to her room, Zollie blamed the mistake on ignorance, saying that his wife had heard the instruction wrong. Then they scurried to correct the error.

It took a great deal of gall for Troop to think himself invincible enough to pass me off as a young woman in need and then risk my saying any variety of things that would expose his past. But he surmised that I would want to protect his wife from any more turmoil. Better, he thought, to let her stay put on her familiar purple divan under the weight of her familiar burden. I would keep the peace and let people think that he had a grateful niece in his employ, that he cared for his wife so dearly that he had put in a special order for just the right sort of young lady, all the way from Washington.

It was clear in his smile that he enjoyed the idea of having me there, supposedly as demeaned as he had felt growing up. He had a member of Toby Greene's inner sanctum present to persecute, tactfully and with menacing efficiency—I was supposed to crumble whenever I looked around this perfect home and saw how happy he was, how well he had done without my grandfather's and mother's love and support. What he could not understand was that my family was too busy thrashing out such matters as whether they could ethically turn away the ghost of Lizzie Borden, whether the heart or the brain was the repository of the soul, why their old friend Dr. Walter Reed had deserved the Nobel Prize more than Sir Ronald Ross, to give a moment's thought to the fact that Troop Ross had nice things and a nice colored woman to dust them. The way we really lived repulsed him more than anything else. His father's authenticity made him draw back in discomfort, as though it were a form of living best left to the bluntly, uninhibitedly retarded. He wanted nothing to do with a spontaneous life, where there was always the threat that one might forget oneself and lose control in an instant of joy or surprise.

My mother wrote several times to make it clear that I was welcome to turn around and go back to Washington, and when I said I would not, she replied:

Then I suggest you try to focus Maureen's mind on the baby. It isn't natural that she is this close and not at least counting off the days and fantasizing about pinafores and frocks. I've enclosed some cute suggestions that your grandmothers and I came up with. Your grandfathers tried to help, but I couldn't send along their list, which included a jar of metal shavings and a magnet, an ant farm, and a monkey. I told Father what's going on down there, and he wanted me to tell you that she can come up here and have the baby, though we all know that Troop will not allow that to happen. Father did say that Maureen is to be admired and given all the love and help she needs. If anything begins to feel, as Grammar used to say, "too wrong," you are to come home immediately, and have her with you. Frankly, I'm amazed that she married him and has stuck with it. Be sure to tell her that we killed Troop's mother from up here, so she can release herself from that responsibility. How she has not been thoroughly disdone by it all is perfectly supernatural.

Mother offered to come to Elm City, but I thought that would make things worse. Her offer did, however, stay in the back of my mind, as a last resort. She also offered to write Maureen a personal note, and I told her that would be fine. I gave Maureen the telephone numbers for both houses in Washington and made sure she understood that she never needed my, or anyone's, permission to call. When I told her about my mother's suggestion that I fix up a Jack Horner welcome corner in her bedroom, she became extremely agitated and said, "No, I'm sorry. Not now. Please. Later. Later is fine." I apologized and said I wouldn't mention anything else about preparations.

"My body," she groaned as she tried to lift her legs onto the chaise. I tried to help, but couldn't because her knees were waterlogged. I sat on the floor and massaged them until they relaxed enough to bend. When she was finally able to rest, she told me, "Mary, I'm supposed to be able to count on you. And so I really mean it, please do not bring anything else into the house about the baby, no ideas. I'm fine about me. To be honest, I'm scared to die but glad for the rest. But you can't tease God about a baby."

She seemed more frustrated by my pressing her to do something she didn't want to do than by the superstition itself. She had to know that I heard her and believed her. She was frustrated by small, fragmented needs that had accrued over the years, from her desire to be heard without a spontaneous challenge to the desire to be touched on her skin rather than through her clothing. Her husband so often told her that her skin felt dirty and tacky to him that she automatically pulled her skirt over her knees when I massaged them, and tugged her blouse up on her shoulder when I touched her there. She assumed that she would always have to justify her need to be shown a little humanity.

"Maureen," I said, "do you know what a joy you are to listen to, to touch?"

"No, and I'm too tired to argue. Maybe one day I'll be that kind of person, but not now."

"Yes, now." I sat beside her and held her sore, bare legs in my lap, wondering how long she would need to be touched and held before she believed in her beauty. I knew I was willing to give her all the time and care she required, but if her husband could've occasionally answered one simple need without demanding a proper regulation request or thanks, he could've settled her spirit, in less time than it had taken him to injure her to begin with. She would have seemed less "hysterical." But she was flatly denied the compassionate understanding that he should have given, free and unencumbered by her certain expectation of his relentless and thorough reprisals. He routinely treated her like a landlord vexed by a shiftless tenant who he feels is abusing his hospitality—although his wife's imperfections did not amount to anything, for she had spent their five years of marriage hectically correcting faults as soon as he brought them to her attention, not to mention attempting to have them "medically" excised. But there was nothing inside her that could blacken her soul or even tarnish it. When I looked through her eyes and into her, past the wounds, what I found there was as decent as I have ever known. What I saw in her truly was what Bancroft meant when he called beauty "the sensible image of the Infinite." But for her to get through even the most quotidian of her days required so much power and dexterity that I thought when I died I would track down whoever has the power to calm a woman's dense and marathon existence and say, "You owe them. Get to it."

Seven

One day I got caught making a sandwich. Mamie rushed over and said, "The last thing you need to do is be slinging a piece of meat between some bread and serving it to yourself. I fixed your lunch, right in there."

"Mamie, you know I appreciate it, but I've been here long enough to want to pick up with some of my own routine. At home, I sit on the sofa with a sandwich and read the newspaper, which I haven't seen since I've been here. I'd like to see what's happening with the war."

"He wants you to stop eating up there," she told me. Then she apologized and closed her eyes to concentrate while she quoted from my uncle's household management guide. "We have lunch on damask and dinner on lace, unless, of course, the damask is colored."

She was enormously relieved when I abandoned the sandwich and went into the parlor, where a tea table was set. "They don't take a newspaper," she said, "but there's books in here if you need to read. Just put them back exactly where you found them. And I thank you for letting go of eating out of your hands."

If a person who knew nothing about my uncle were to look at the framed grade-school report from his early years in Washington that hung on his study wall, the person would assume that a glad independence of mind and spirit was treasured in this place. Reading my grandfather into the teacher's words, I still could not understand what would warrant Nora's having taken her child away from his beneficial influence. I stood in the study and read it again:

> *Young Master Troop knows what needs to be done and does it. It is unfortunate, however, that he be lashed to the name "Troop" for the rest of his life, for he will never consent to march with one. He may face some difficulty in manhood keeping steady with the sometimes rather intense singularity of himself. When lesser men with more measured strides seem to succeed better and faster, he must choose whether to join an ordinary race or follow the arc of his creative will to better and higher glory. But come what may, to himself and his Episcopal God he will be true.*

This was how he had preserved the memory of who he was before his spirit was broken. He was obviously proud of it. I thought he should have tacked up a commentary beside it: "Yes, I'm aware that the boy described here is not me anymore. I lost him, and I'm afraid. I think I may be a terrible fraud now. I miss him, but I'm ashamed to search for him. Maybe I should treat my wife better for having to endure me. Will you show me how?"

While I waited for Mamie to bring the food in, I telephoned the newspaper and arranged for a daily delivery. Mamie must have heard me, and coming in, she said, "You hadn't ought to of done that. Mr. Ross gets all his news outside the house. I'm just not used to anybody in the house having a need of knowing what's happening."

I sat down and let her serve me. "There's too much going on in the world for me to be sitting here alone eating a heart-of-palm salad."

"I know," Mamie said. "I certainly do. It's terrible, but he doesn't like the world coming in the house." She told me that she would collect the newspapers from the yard each morning and bring them to my room. And then she thanked me and said, "You're good for her. All she needs is somebody kind and that can stand up." She also asked whether I might slip her the newspapers after I was through with them. Zollie was learning to read, and it was a struggle, she told me, owing to both his responsibilities and his sense of dignity. She had been teaching him from *The Eclectic First Reader,* but he was often so embarrassed to hear his deep voice reading aloud about the little boy who couldn't go out to play because he ate too much cake or the little girl who lost her goat that he would invent reasons to end a day's lessons. He had recently claimed to be compelled to bleach the floor of the chicken house rather than learn the vocabulary words at the end of a story about a lonesome peg-legged man. "My husband," Mamie told me, "could not bear it, so I thank you for bringing him the news."

That autumn, all over the world, people were doing just this, bringing one another the news of the day—the peaceful world promised in Wilson's "Fourteen Points," the miracles of Harry Houdini and Henry Ford, the breaking of the Hindenburg Line, how a French family was treating somebody's housekeeper's nephew like a prince while he recovered in their home. A person couldn't ride the trolleys without hearing horror stories of heads being blown off and collecting in the trenches; heads and bodies being shipped home in confused caskets; eyelids peeling back from gas; burning, baking, blistering skin. There was restrained debate over whether death in an ignoble battle with an unpronounceable name, over a plot of ground no wider than a grave, was worth the country's having given up the peace.

Nothing, though, was said about the war in my aunt and uncle's household. Coming there from Washington was much like moving to a neutral country. I had left the busy wartime life of the capital but also the sustained patriotic fervor that my grandparents carried out across the street. They had ordered all the flags they could from the embassies of the Allied nations and hung them like window shades across the front of their house. What flags couldn't be gotten they pieced together like quilts on the kitchen floor. When there was good news from overseas, they would open the windows and bang out patriotic tunes on the piano. I was sent to North Carolina with an extra American flag, but it lay ignored on the foyer table until Mamie and Zollie hung it by the entrance door.

My uncle had them remove it immediately. "This isn't anything I would expect you to have known," he told me, "but people of quality don't *show* themselves this blatantly. It tends toward the vulgar. Better to leave it to barbershops and public buildings."

"My grandfather would be surprised to hear that his patriotism's vulgar," I replied.

"We are talking about the same man who frolics about at those free-love events. Am I right?"

"We are," I told him, "but there's a difference."

"And I'm not inclined to listen to it."

That's how all of my early conversations with Troop ended. If he sensed the approach of something he did not want to deal with, any emotional disarray, he dismissed me or left. At times I suspected that he didn't care whether Germany prevailed, for one of the things he admired most was the relentless pursuit of Teutonic ideals, excellence, order, and perfection. The war didn't affect the household with any excitement or fear, because it was made to be respectfully discreet and keep its problems to itself. He never railed against

Wilson, but I did hear him remark to a business associate that Henry Ford had been a fool to waste good money to, as he said, "finance that vapid peace cruise with those freethinking idiots." The word "free" attached to almost any word could be counted on to revolt him—freethinking, freewheeling, free-loving, and I suppose free-falling, all implied a dangerous level of personal irresponsibility.

Troop brought his household no news from the outside, nothing regarding what his business associates were saying at the office, and nobody asked. After a few weeks, I thought that if I connected a question to his life, his concerns, he might answer it. I found him at the dining room table at four o'clock one morning. He was dressed casually, it being a Saturday. His usual manner of business attire was, like his regulated house, out of the last century, and when he relaxed in clothing that was just a tad shiny or shabby, he favored an absurd butler in a costume drama who goes about in his late master's suits.

He asked what I was doing up, and I told him that I was going to the kitchen to hunt down ginger root for Aunt Maureen's nausea.

He muttered, "More high drama," and returned to his documents.

When I came back through the dining room with the ginger root, I stopped and said, "She feels rotten. She hasn't slept well all night."

"Then that should help." That was evidently all he intended to say.

"I was wondering if the Duke brothers' tobacco concern

had been affected by the war," I said, thinking that I would hear bluntly that it either was or was not, and would then go to my aunt.

He responded, "I really can't say," and resumed his work and the meal that had made Mamie miss her ride home with Zollie and spend the night at the house for the one purpose of preparing it long before dawn. I thought Maureen would not be ill served by my delaying returning to her long enough to force him to say.

I asked, "Is it that you're prohibited from speaking about the European trade, or that you won't?"

"I won't."

"If you think you'd be wasting your time because I wouldn't understand, that's just not the case," I said.

"No, Mary, I know you would understand. But do you not see this work? Do you not wonder why I might be up this early?"

I apologized for being intrusive. "I misunderstood the tone."

"What tone?"

"Your voice, the way you tend to speak."

"And how is that?"

"Hard."

"It's interesting that I'm in my home before dawn with a guest and being told something so utterly without basis that I'm without any kind of response. You've inherited a low opinion of me, Mary, and listening to it rather makes me wonder if you also inherited any notion of the sort of respect due one's host."

His tone had worsened, but entangling myself further

served absolutely no purpose. "Never mind. I shouldn't have stopped anyway, not with Maureen upstairs spewing last night's stuffed peppers into the wastepaper basket."

He left his plate on the table, gathered his papers and his driver, and prepared to leave. Zollie had been in the kitchen with Mamie since three. He had left the children alone at two-thirty in the morning and driven thirty minutes over dirt and macadam roads so he could take his employer the ten blocks to his office. Zollie's sister, who sounded too imbecilic to be watching children, could not get to their house until six, because she could not tell time and depended on others to awaken her. When her children were left alone like this, Mamie was nervous all day, worrying at their being able to get ready for school. She was anxious about their safety as well as the possibly missed lessons. Their subscription school, run at her church, was in session for only the three months of the year when the older students were not involved with planting, tending, and harvesting crops. Then the minister expected students in the classroom on many evenings and Saturdays—Mamie complied, she said, for fear that her boys would "always be running woefully behind the rest of the human race." I did not see many opportunities for Mamie and Zollie to sleep more than five hours a night.

One would think that a man who has set such a long string of inconveniences in motion would at least send some roses to the housekeeper. It is reasonable that a man who puts people out in such an extreme way, be they the colored help or not, would be careful in his encounters with them. He would lie low. But my uncle was able to provoke those he had encroached upon, unfazed that anyone might take offense when he snatched whatever he saw as critical to his own sustenance, chiefly the time and deference ordinarily due women and children.

When Aunt Maureen was better and sleeping, I went downstairs and helped Mamie fold laundry. "Is anything going on with Uncle Troop outside the house?" I asked her.

"I wondered when you were going to ask something like that," she said. "But it isn't anything you think. It isn't anybody else but himself."

I was holding letters for Washington, and when I asked whether I should take them to the post office or leave them in the mailbox beside the car porch, she told me, "You put them in the mailbox, although 'car porch' tends to go by 'porte cochere.' Well, more than tends to. It better should. And just in case you call your front parlor the front parlor at your own house, here it needs to go by 'drawing room.' One more thing, Mary. Mr. Troop may turn the other cheek if you slip up and call his porte cochere a car porch and his drawing room a front parlor, but do not *ever* say 'house.' He has to have it 'home.'"

His determination both to sound correct and to impose a certain sympathetic appeal onto the place by forcing us all to say, for instance, "The home needs dusting," was propped at a ludicrous angle to good sense, etiquette, and truth, and I could not do it. Mamie and Zollie did, but it was one of the many things they had stopped hearing themselves say. Aunt

Maureen could make do mainly with the word "here," as she so rarely left it.

At every turn, I remembered how I had visualized what my life in this house, or home, would be, when I had thought Maureen would be the kind of woman who bustles about with the household keys attached to a large ring on her belt. After the baby's arrival, I imagined, she would sit alert on a satin slipper chair, scribbling orders on a pad while a large colored nurse brought an infant in for hurried viewings. I would be an emotionally and financially stable Lily Bart in *The House of Mirth*, going about town, placing cards on small silver trays held in the outstretched hands of a dozen or so butlers, organizing her return to her regular rounds of visitation at the first decent moment. I thought she would be going and doing incessantly, whipping things into shape, and then she would stand on the landing and languidly ask the servants not to bang about during her routine retreat, when she would take off her shoes, lie down in her clothes. I would cover her with a blue or pink satin afternoon quilt and see her again on the other side of a deep and instant sleep. But the reality was that she did nothing all day but exist from one minute to the next on air that seemed begrudgingly meted out in portions so small she could barely keep enough force pushed together to sustain her very polite melancholy.

It was the middle of October when she said to me, "Mary, sometimes, you know, I wonder if I haven't already died, and none of this means anything. I could either be living or just way inside the memory of living. Do you know?"

I said, "You're alive, and you'll stay that way."

After this, I stopped going to my room to sleep. I lay on the wide chaise with her and listened to her breathing, and I watched her chest and her baby, rising and sinking regularly, until I was sure she was asleep. Although I tried to stay close to her when Troop was home, sometimes he took the opportunity of just a few minutes with her alone to tell her what had been on his mind that day. I opened her door one evening, having been gone five minutes, and found him at the foot of the chaise, saying, "Do you think you're competent to take care of a baby, Maureen? Are you capable? Can you be in charge of another life after you've made this lamentable mess of your own? Or are you going to make demands on me and try to interfere with my life and my time the way you did with my mother?"

I waited for him in the hall and said, "You've said my family's responsible for your mother's death, and now you accuse your wife. Did the woman die twice? The rest of the world has to face facts. Why are you entitled to these flagrant misinterpretations of reality?"

He smiled. "No, you're the one who is misinterpreting facts. I was only making a point with Maureen."

"What kind of point is made like that?"

"This is none of your concern," he said, "but you can either believe the truth or her version of it. My mother was made to wait for me to come to dinner at her house because Maureen delayed me over some trivia, and frankly, she never recovered. Unless you've forgotten your family history, I was all she had."

When I asked Maureen about the nature of the trivia that had delayed him, she told me she had tripped on the sidewalk and broken her ankle. She had sent for Troop, and he had picked her up and dropped her off at his doctor's house. He helped her to the door and left her there, grousing without cease about how his mother was waiting and no doubt worried sick over where he was, how the meal she had prepared with "her own tired hands" was getting cold. And then Maureen begged me not to tell him what she'd said.

The question of what he would do, what consequences would result from all of her various trespasses, came into my head and wouldn't leave. But I was never afraid he would kill her outright. My fear was that he would somehow make her be dead. Not that I worried she would commit suicide. She would die, I thought, by an overdose of this passively cruel neglect, an attitude nursed by his fear. He controlled and abandoned the household simultaneously—a feat of accomplishment for one person to orchestrate and sheer terror for the inhabitants to live through.

The day after I quizzed him about his twice dead mother, he brought a few people from his company over to meet me. I imagined it as some kind of diabolical plot he had devised overnight to punish me, but I still hoped that some things in the household were nothing more than what they were described to be. Although he said that he had given me notice of the visit on several occasions, I knew that he had not. There was no question of Maureen's going downstairs for this cocktail hour, but she encouraged me to "look nice and not be late." So, assuming that this house dressed for the smallest gatherings, I changed into the closest thing I had to a gown, and hoped that a marcasite necklace would lend me what people were calling "the look." But I was always just one octave away from that, continually perplexed by what missing link from the pages of the fashion magazines might give me the polish and finish that seemed inbred in other young women. Yet I was also afraid that I'd fall short of the archetypal socially deprived match girl Troop had encouraged them to expect.

When I reached the parlor, eight or nine people were regarding the pug by the hearth and advising my uncle on what should be the length of its tenure before it was traded for an Italian greyhound, the current rage. Troop introduced me around, simply and tactfully, and then continued dilating on the bone structure of greyhounds. He meant to convey a studied indifference to these domestic matters. But the only effect it had on me was to make me want to march right back upstairs and ask Maureen to please explain why in God's name she had married this man who now seemed to want to purchase a racehorse of a dog to tear through her house. He looked pleased with his decision to wait until the right breeder could be found. I found myself nodding in agreement. His smile was definitely a draw, and seeing it at work so well let me know that although it, and the big bright teeth, were certainly not the reason she married him, they must have influenced her decision to give him more than the first ten minutes of her hard-earned time.

He appeared to be working around to something, some memorable kernel that would define this cocktail hour and make it and him the subject of a week or more of the guests' amazed admiration. He stood in front of the hearth and said he wanted to tell a little story to help welcome Miss Mary Oliver into his home. He had my attention.

He said: "I knew a man in Winston, when I was first associated with the Duke brothers, but working in a more personal, daily capacity. And my God, this man had no peace. Poor fellow ended up shooting himself in the chest a few years ago. It was terrible. The Dukes rode him constantly. And we had no idea why at first, except that he had five or six children and a freethinker for a wife, who believed that hiring servants perpetuated the woes of the underclass. The rest of us went about with a lean and hungry look and fought to get ahead and stay that way. But this fellow, he put in his nine and left. He was the servant. He was the nigger help. It was he who was the boy in his own home. And he had mass potential, triple the mass potential of the rest of us. He would have made a bully director, but he was in a quandary. The Duke brothers knew which way his decision should have fallen, though they did not make a habit of interfering with a man's home life. He confided in the rest of us, as people tend to do when they feel themselves mired in a hopeless situation. That says a great deal about what was lacking in his character, besides a thorough want of pride. He had to try and drag us down with him. Well, push came to shove when his wife announced she was expecting another one. I think he just could not reconcile himself to brushing out milk bottles of an evening when he should have been with the rest of us, burning the midnight oil. And then he was found like that, shot in the chest."

The guests' eyes fell on me at once, silently thanking me for taking care of Maureen, doing that particular heavy lifting, submitting myself to the freaks of her temper so that her husband wouldn't have to shoot himself. He didn't look at me, but he brought a shoal of gentlemen over to where I stood. He'd turned to the topic of marriage, and the conversation moved across the room with them.

He concluded that the ideal marriage was "a quid pro quo sort of arrangement," and he regretted that in discussing professional ambitions versus family planning with the young moderns he had interviewed recently for some openings with Mr. Duke, they didn't appear to take him seriously when he advised that they consider a bride an important purchase they would be paying both principal and interest on for some time.

He boasted that he didn't hire those whose youthful idealism was still intact, not yet uprooted by the commercial mentality of a cynic. "You either buy, barter, trade, or sell," he said. "I warn those boys that no union is free. They tend to run a great deal more than the cake and the costumes. And I can't hire the ones who married beneath themselves. When I tell them what an asset a wife can be, they drone on about being in love, and I remind them what all these young moderns have forgotten. It's what women have always known, and that is the fact that love isn't at all necessary in an ambitious marriage. But they can't be told anything."

If that was true, then his union with my aunt was a usurious arrangement that profited him enormously, but he wouldn't rest until he had wiped her account clean of everything she had. He craved her spiritual position much more than she desired his social one, but he would've mocked any suggestion that measuring station and position might be a hazardous method for a man or a woman to reckon personal worth. And then he came to resent the authentic gifts she had given him as dowry—honesty, compassion, intelligence, beauty, empathy, hope—but he hadn't minded pillaging them, leaving her spent, as though she were suffering from some wasting disease of the soul.

By the time I got to Elm City, my uncle was deep into what seemed something of a mechanical process of turning against Maureen. He was methodical, and thus she missed even the passionate sensation of an explosion, something immense and purgative that would then require a period of silence, regretful memory of their mutual regard, and either a reunion or a blunt decision to live separate lives in opposite wings of the house. The purging could have been something almost wholesome that would get it out and set the record straight, but he did not see her as worth the effort. And it would've been too unsightly and loud for him. When I went upstairs after the cocktail party, Maureen was in a trancelike sleep on her back. As I watched, the child kicked time and time again, hard, as if trying to knock over the traces that bound the two of them. The baby was pounding at the walls, wanting out now, having no doubt heard and seen so much already through the thin veil of drum-tight skin that this probably looked like the best thing to do, to get out as soon as possible and grow tall enough to stand between a father and a mother.

Eight

A fragile loveliness can wither if the adoration of a man disappears. A woman's strength can atrophy if her husband stops believing in her, and in her exhausted resignation she will sigh her way through the most routine days. Beauty of face and figure is designed to be ephemeral and tends by nature to leave slowly over the years, but I knew a woman whom it abandoned overnight, when she realized she was without the love she was promised at the altar. She was my mother's closest friend, even though she lived in New York. Instead of writing Maureen an encouraging note, Mother sent me two of her friend's letters and suggested that I read them to Maureen. "Tell her about the extraordinary life and death and life of Judith Benedict," she said, "and see if she doesn't find some inspiration in that. If not, throw your hands up over the situation and rob the house on the way out so it won't seem so much like a bad waste of time."

Love, my mother believed, was the only specific for true beauty—an abundance of it could make a woman who was as plain as zwieback go into the streets smiling, with her head high and her shoulders back, and a dearth of it could trans-figure a good and glowing aspect into one that drove the woman to lock herself away like a vampire. As for my mother, she appears in her wedding photograph to be a handsome woman, with a healthy body and a furnished mind, the type of woman who is assumed to be responsible, efficient, and kind to animals and old people; but it was my father's adora-tion and then the memory of it that elevated her to a dear and perfect splendor. And she was never aware that I knew how she made sure she stayed that way.

She took for granted that intelligence was needed. She be-lieved that a woman had to be bright enough to choose cor-rectly and distinguish between abiding trust and transient infatuation. She believed also that a woman's intelligence, which she called "the ability and desire to spend as much time in the world of serious ideas as in the shoe shop," should be swirled in with her other attributes. She spoke of intelli-gence as heightening the impact a woman could make, the way a cook might scare vanilla batter with just enough nut-meg to make the cake memorable.

She explained that the optimal situation involves heart and mind working together, and that only a woman who is swept away could be ignorant of the way the heart was always pressing for advantages behind the mind's back. "The heart is a metaphor for the soul," she told me. "The soul wants to feel good all the time. Feeling good all the time is irresponsible. And someone must be hurt in order for that to happen. The heart will inevitably find you the most all-around charming man in the room, but you should never trust it to decide if he should be kept. The heart throws no fish back in the river. It doesn't realize that there is always another one coming around the bend."

Before September of 1918, I had met only one woman, my mother's friend Judith Benedict, whose ordeal in love approached the misery of my aunt's. Common sense was available to tell me what to do, but it would work only as far as my uncle let it. I was never so glad to see anything as I was those letters from her friend that my mother sent to North Carolina. She had no idea how many times I had already read them.

After my father and brother died, Mother and I made frequent trips to New York to pick up the threads that had been dropped when my father's illnesses and Daniel's troubles denied her the continued luxury of visiting old friends. We were always met in the lobby of the Waldorf for afternoon tea by Judith Benedict Stafford, a lady of phenomenal beauty and immaculate manner whom my mother described as highly original and just as appropriate. My impression of her when I was small was that she was human perfection, and even when I saw her after time had passed, I was still in awe.

In my seventeenth year, the last time Mrs. Stafford would

meet us at the hotel, an old gentleman approached and stood before our table, locked in a spasm of bewilderment that did not abate until she told him very gently that although the attention was flattering, she should not neglect my mother and me. He asked if he might touch her garment anyway. "Otherwise," he said, "I will strangle on my own misery."

Mother asked what it was like to have one's face and form cause such commotion, and Mrs. Stafford leaned in to us, poked my mother on the knee, and said, "I know I'm not supposed to enjoy it, but I secretly do." She said that she was fortunate all around. Everything was a blessing.

We were at home no more than a month when Mrs. Stafford sent Mother a letter that was so quickly shoved into a hatbox on a far shelf that I was compelled to retrieve it. This I did while my mother was across the street consulting my grandparents, and I then began a secretive involvement in Mrs. Stafford's secret life that preoccupied me until I read the letter she would eventually send from Europe. In this one, she said she had found the answers to the important questions of a woman's life, and she thanked my mother for showing her the way. Although she and I never spoke of it, the route for my mother led through a suite on the top floor of the Jefferson Hotel that she had been keeping since the third anniversary of my father's death.

I didn't know whether or where Maureen would find her joy and will. I wasn't sure that adequate hope could be born with a child. But Mrs. Stafford had found her joy and will, and so had my mother. Mrs. Stafford had to exile herself from this country, and my mother had only to take the trolley to the Jefferson Hotel, but they had both managed their salvation, and they were both thriving.

I waited until Maureen had finished a stack of hand sewing that had been on her mind to explain why my mother had sent Mrs. Stafford's letters. I told her about the tea at the Waldorf, how blessed the woman felt to have everything in her life exactly where it needed to be. Before I could say anything else, Maureen asked, "And then what happened to her?"

I handed her the first letter, and said, "This." We sat there and read together what my mother's friend had told her six years before.

May 3, 1912

My dear, kind Martha,

This was a shock to me, and it will be to you, which I say so that you do not think that I was hiding any truth or being careful in Mary's company. (Although I would have been, for it is not fit to be told.) I cannot believe that it was five weeks ago that we were together. This morning makes an hour seem like a year. I have been staggered beyond the human capacity for staggering. Perhaps when I tell you what happened, some of the outrage will leave me. It is so bad that I lay down to try to sleep a short while ago, and in the five minutes I managed to stay out, I dreamed there was a life's worth of nightmares.

Remember when we were girls together? Remember when we were at Barnard? We planned a love match and swore never to settle for less. I had it, and now it is gone. Not to say that my husband has died, though if he jumped off the roof today, I would reach down, get his billfold, and walk on. Sorry to sound this way, but he has already taxed my sympathy enough.

After I returned from a dental appointment this morning, I found him in my bed with a tubercular-looking little tramp. Yesterday, this same creature accosted me twice on the street in front of the house. She gets people coming and going. I told her I'd already bought a box of matches from her the day before, and she set up the most loathsome, taunting tirade behind my back. "The Princess has everything she needs! She does, does she?" And on and on.

She did not look to have the energy to be doing what she was doing to him, but she did, which means that whatever venereal corruption was consuming her had taken a holiday and left her to enjoy some strength, because I will tell you that he looked to be dying more from pure physical exertion than the shock of my opening the door.

He said right off that it was not his fault—but this woman-child did not force entry into my home and neither was she alone underneath those new Frette linens. He said that I brought this upon myself by ceasing to give him the attention I used to. And he let her listen to this. (God only knows what she gave him besides attention.) Martha, this may have been the worst of it, how he let her hear this, how he said it with my name. He said "Judith" in front of her. He may as well have touched her breasts right there with me watching as let her hear the intimacy of my name.

Everything is fouled. My favorite robe, the one you and Mary sent from Paris for my birthday, was hanging off her. I hope you do not mind, but I told the bitch to take it. You know it had to be soaked with their gore, and the thought of putting my hands to it even to throw it away made me sick. I couldn't.

I told them both they should die. Then I got the fireplace matches off the hearth, the ones I had bought from her, and I struck one and gave them silently to know I would burn them alive before he said another thing about me in front of this mean little urchin.

I said, "You're both common," and then he had the gall to use his pet name for me, "Princess." The last I'd heard it was yesterday, out of her mouth, on the street.

He told me he was always careful of the neighbors when she came over. "It isn't like I've flaunted her in your face, Princess."

I said, "So you've had her in my bed and then let me sleep in it at night. This is the most sordid, the most vulgar thing I've ever heard of. Do you think I'm that filthy or that worthless?"

Martha, I will never be able to get over this, not unless somebody helps me by holding him down on the floor and letting me beat him about the head and neck with my hands. I can feel the need in my arms.

He had every attribute of a dog except fidelity. I knew this happened on his trips abroad, but this is my home. This is the place I made for us. Part of me wanted to drag the bed out to the sidewalk and hang a sign on it saying

"Desecrated." Instead, I packed a few things with the two of them lying there watching, and then I left. I went immediately to the bank and withdrew every penny possible, and then I checked into a sunny room at the Waldorf. I had them send up a roasted chicken and some candy and a chocolate milk shake.

I have lain in one spot all day, feeling alternately disoriented and alert, composed. You know I had always wanted children, but if I had that additional pressure right now, I think I would lapse into a durable and absolute state of catatonia. This may be the longest afternoon of my life.

I have read enough to know that I must prove abandonment to have any legal relief, but how do I do that when I am the one leaving? What I may need first is for you to please help me get to my family in Baltimore. Yes, there are people here, but I am not of a mind to involve them. They'll know more than I do soon enough. Talking is their life.

What did your mother once say of divorce? The public airing of private grievances, and so the better to shoot each other at home and hire out to the attorneys only when the time comes to drag the corpses through the street?

So I close now and think of you,

Fondly, warmly, with love,

Judith

After we finished reading the letter, Maureen asked, "What happened next and then next?"

I told her what happened during the period my family called "Judith's interlude." Mother collected her from New York and brought her to Washington to rest with us before she took her on to Baltimore. Mrs. Stafford was destroyed. Had I not read her letter before Mother walked her through the door, I would have wondered whether a madman had just subjected her to some bizarre facial surgery. Her face was clawed by disappointment and nervous hives. Welts that had healed unevenly gave her skin the appearance of having been sloppily basted together in patches, like a poorly made scrap quilt. Her lashes were almost all missing—her eyes looked like they had been broiled inside their sockets, not unlike my grandfather's after the occasional electromagnetic mishap. A stranger would've wondered whether she had been stabbing at her lips with the tips of a fountain pen, so persistently had she been biting them, and there was an angry, infected mass where she had chewed through to her gum. She was ashamed to go to the doctor, so she futilely caked the sore with a vile-smelling patent unguent.

"But," she told us, "I've been able to stop what had been a continual stream of tears, because these little damages turn into caustic horrors when the salt hits them. That's as much self-improvement as I've been able to accomplish."

It was an astonishing vision of willingness and trust, how my mother diverted Mrs. Stafford's attention with risqué songs and jokes while she drained the lip with a hot needle, which she said she would do and which she did do each morning, "so that my oldest friend can, at the very least, walk away from this marriage with her mouth."

The Victoria lace Mrs. Stafford wore pulled down from her hat only heightened the sense of mystery about her and emphasized that she was attempting to hide something grue-some underneath. When she lifted the lace to kiss my grand-parents, she rushed to tell them, "I know. People think I'm hiding the plague or some kind of scrofula or that I've been beaten about the face. And I know how the rest of my head looks, but this isn't my hair. I have Chinese hair now. Mine fell out last week in these wadding heaps, and now my teeth are loose, but I suppose I have to tell myself, 'That's just the way of the world.'"

Grandmother Louise spoke directly to Mrs. Stafford, ig-noring everything that was being discussed around her. "Ju-dith, what are you planning to say to your mother? Have you thought about how to talk to her? What does she know? I ask because we had a late supper with her a few months ago, when she and your aunt came into town to see the new play at Ford's Theatre, and she did not look well. I believe you should give this some thought."

Mrs. Stafford said that although she was aching to go to her old home, she wasn't aching to tell her mother the truth. She would have her believe that she had some generalized physi-cal debility, and that my mother had insisted she be evaluated at a hospital in Baltimore.

Grandmother Louise, who had known Mrs. Stafford about as long as my mother had, said, "But Judith, you look like a ghoul. Your mother may tell you to skip the hospital and re-port to the mortuary."

Mrs. Stafford was too preoccupied by the deep and serious

truth of the news to be insulted. She repeated that she would have to lie to her mother, and then eventually, when the time was right, when her mother would not be as upset, she would tell her the truth.

My grandmother was rattled by this plan. "You intend to wait until she has died to be honest with her? Or do you plan to let her die thinking that you and your husband are just not spending a great deal of time together?"

My mother took up her friend's part. "I'll help Judith sort this out when we get to Baltimore."

"Martha, you aren't exactly the person to trust on matters of subterfuge," said Grandmother Louise.

"What do you mean?" Mother wanted to know.

"What have you ever been able to hide from me? What can any daughter hide? Judith, your mother will not need to be told anything but the smallest details. A woman can see damage done to her child. Don't dishonor a mother with a silly and futile lie."

No one knew that I knew the details, that I had read the letter. All I was given to know was that her husband had left her and there had been a scene. Anyone looking at the devastation could assume the humiliation had been agonizing, to cut and gouge at her beauty as it did.

Mrs. Stafford decided to tell her mother the truth about what had become of her. She didn't need the lie festering on her lips, which had come almost back into their natural form in the weeks my mother had kept them drained and nourished with aloe from the kitchen windowsill. She was not going to lie to her mother, and she wasn't going to wait until she saw her to start speaking the truth. She told anyone who might inquire after her husband back in New York, "Oh, I'm not married anymore. I'm getting divorced. It was just best that I leave."

Three weeks before she went to Baltimore, my grandparents arranged a demonstration by their favorite palm reader and a performance by a Hindu levitation expert as an evening's diversion for her. I walked around offering a tray of stale pastries to a large and vivid mix of professors, senators' and ambassadors' wives, and amateur spiritualists. At the end of the night, Mrs. Stafford thanked my family and the guests, saying that everyone had made her feel uncommonly embraced. Then she removed her veil and turned her body toward the unmistakably enamored Hindu performer. They had spent much of the evening talking. I overheard her tell Mother, "The levitationist is devastating. Listen to me. That's certainly not anything I thought I'd ever hear myself say."

When Maureen had thanked us, he removed one of the scarves from his waist and tenderly wrapped it around her head, stood back, and said, "To consume the lady is all my heart requires to relieve my sorrowful hunger," and then he stunned us all even more with a pledge of "permanent devotion to the most beautiful mortal mind and flesh alive."

I recalled what the old man at the Waldorf had said about strangling on his misery. I asked myself, as my mother had asked Mrs. Stafford that day when I was too young to divine the mesmerizing power of such a blunt force of nature as she was, how it would feel to be the object of so much sensual devouring.

Until she left for Baltimore, she would walk on her own for hours, in sun or rain, and then return, carrying in her clothing the inevitable scent of curry. Eventually, she gained a lucrative divorce that was based, in the main, on affidavits she had found the power and will to pursue from several aggrieved, tubercular-looking match girls who had been promised Fifth Avenue and champagne by her husband but instead got a high-class dose of syphilis and sulfa medication.

She began to travel and did not stop. Before she finally concentrated her fascination on the major cities of Europe, she sent Mother letters, postcards, and thoughtful bibelots from exotic and politically nervous places that she confidently described as "far less treacherous than home." During that early phase of her journeys, she also told Mother that she had at last found the right question, which was necessary to have before she looked for the right answer. "I asked myself, very simply," she wrote, "if the life I had been living was the one I wanted to live. It wasn't. I wanted to be loved and I wanted to be free. If that could not be found, I realized that I would have to be happy alone. And I thank God every day for the money. Even the most imperious hobo still sleeps on the ground."

Nine

Maureen said, "Look outside, Mary. My father hated it when the day stayed rude like this. We lived in a very black, loamy section of the Delta, and when it was like this, he knew he wouldn't be able to get into the fields for days. He'd become agitated. He'd pace. And then he'd go out to the shelters and find something to do until things were dry. He could not sit. My mother used to say this weather was good for only two things, sleeping and reading *Wuthering Heights,* and then she would say, 'Alas, I must clean the house.' She loved to read, but managed only about two books a year. There were seven of us, all girls."

"Is that why you married him? To get out of that?"

"Yes, I will have to say I did. But I loved him. And I thought I would also pull them all out of it, quickly. But Troop begrudged every penny I sent, even a birthday card with a five-dollar bill in it. He counted it all up and said I had to earn it back."

"How? Were you still working then?"

"No, but I owed him fifty-seven dollars nonetheless. And then I got my back up and refused to do it. He reminds me every now and then. Mamie and Zollie heard about this and offered to have it taken out of their pay, but he claimed to have no idea what they were talking about. He still sometimes sees something he wants to buy and tells me he could do it were it not for the fact that my family drank up all that money."

"They don't drink, do they?"

"No."

"Do you want me to give you the money? I will."

"No. He wants it, but it would shame him to take it. You can't win like this, not ever. He'll take you around and around and have you too flustered to think straight, and then he'll call your confusion to your attention. My mother saw this coming. She knows Troop. I promised I would do whatever was within my power to help my family once we were married. The story is that I tried and failed, and now I don't hear from her. But I write anyway, two or three times a week. A couple of years ago, when there was nothing in the mail for a week or so, I even started giving Troop the letters to make sure his secretary got them correctly in the mail. I wondered if I was doing something wrong or just stupidly. And then I wondered if he was keeping the mail on both ends, but I'd tell myself that people don't do that kind of thing."

"Well, they do," I told her. "And that's exactly what has happened here. He did this to you. Think about it, Maureen."

Her eyes said she had suspected the extent of his duplicity for a long time. Perhaps it had been too awful a prospect to face alone, and the presence of someone willing to raise her and to hold her while she contemplated this awful, new estimate of her husband's gall and perfidy was all she needed. She was not an ignorant woman. She was not weak. She was intelligent and strong enough to use whatever lies, half-truths, and denials available to construct a world she could survive this long, and I could only imagine the terror she felt when she took my hand and whispered, "He went too far with my mother, didn't he? A man can't do that to his wife, can he?"

"I wouldn't know how to forgive it. If I were you, I wouldn't know where to begin, like Mrs. Stafford that morning, standing at the foot of her own bed."

"Me, either," said Maureen. "I won't forgive this. I don't want to face him, but he has to know. Everything here seems so damn needlessly cruel. It's like he lives hell-bent on revenge, but I don't know why."

I told her how I believed that a woman's heart can find ways to accustom itself to injury so that a fresh blow would have to be incalculably exquisite or ingeniously delivered to do her new, real harm. By the time I reached her, she was shielding herself every few minutes of the day with such rare materials as are seldom used more than once or twice in a lifetime. She always had to be the foolish virgin, spending her honor, hope, pity, courage, and compassion as though these virtues were infinitely funded. Whether she had known and denied the truth hardly mattered, because the moment she was able to see that her husband had tried to isolate her from her mother, those virtues were back. They were all available to her. He may have been ingenious, but he was now working against feminine instincts that were returning to her with such terrific force that she might have said, "Mary, let's go ahead and have this baby this afternoon." And I would've boiled the water. She was already beginning to think concretely about what was practical for her to attempt at that moment, what could be accomplished without planning, what required contemplation. But she was still fatigued. Her mind was more willing to go and do than her body.

"Just let me hear what happened to Mrs. Stafford," she told me. "That's everything I can manage."

April 24, 1915
My dear Martha,

Prepare to split this letter into installments for later or find an easy place to sit, with good light. Thank goodness I've been cadging from hotel stationery all over Europe. I'm sorry for the length, but there is so very much to say. I want to tell you the things I've decided about my life, and then I want you to bear with me and listen without hat-

ing me for having the audacity to suggest a decision I think you should make about yours.

I told you in the letter I sent from Cuba, when I was on the way to France, that I had decided the life I'd been living wasn't what I wanted. I didn't know what the life I wanted looked like, but I know now that it is one that is as free as I can manage without fear of being hurt. If I don't want to be hurt, I can't put myself in the path where it's likely to happen to me. You would tell Mary not to linger in dark alleys in downtown Washington for fear of her being attacked, that it's more likely to happen there than if she were out in broad daylight on a busy thoroughfare. It's the same thing. I'm likely to be hurt when I'm with people I don't want to be with and doing things I don't want to do. This is not selfishness, as in getting my way, but doing what I want to do, granting myself my own choices on the things that matter in a life.

But there are the small things, too, like putting milk in my tea after I've avoided it for years because of the way my husband would take the pitcher out of my hand, saying it reminded him of someone he knew in college whose silly English affectations irritated him. I stopped saying that I liked the milk and that what he remembered with displeasure from college didn't involve me. But since I realized the urgent importance of doing my life my way, I've practically been swimming in a river of milk.

Martha, life is a river, and don't laugh at me for sounding simpleminded and trite. I know how you are. But life is a river, and I am not on it so much as I am in it. Life is all around me all the time, and what I think has gone wrong—memories that plague me, I don't want to destroy them. Now I know, you see, that everything is in the river with me, even the hate and the blame, and it all makes me who I am, and it has taken me off the banks of the river and pulled me down into the water, where we belong.

Now I understand what your dear father Toby meant when he said he tells the ghosts, "Nothing stops." It keeps flowing, and we ultimately become what we truly are, some sooner than others. So, please pass along to him that I'm finally having my cake and eating it, too, for once I realized that I want to love and be loved as strongly as I want to be free, I was able to figure out how to do it. Please tell him that I am now living what I wanted to be.

Practical hearts like yours need to know about processes and procedures, and it is, for now, as simple as this. I've gotten to know some men, Martha. All various shapes and sizes of men. The one rule is that I don't remain with them if anything makes me sad or afraid. I can love, and I can get up and leave. If I wake up and don't look forward to the day ahead of me, I can create a different one. I'm not trapped and dragged through days and the years with a husband, like mine was, with his whores and his insults.

We stay together, these men and I, and I've yet to be cast out of a hotel or looked at as though I'm plying a trade. It's different in Europe, particularly in France. Puritanism doesn't exist here. The ones with that bent have long since left for New England. There's nothing dirty or Bohemian about it. The man sleeping six feet from me right now is a

London professor, in Paris for the year. It isn't one of those cases where the American woman poses for a painter and things go from there.

I don't "pick them up," but neither can I tell you exactly how it happens. All I know is that once I realized the possibility of having love with the freedom, I saw that it may be unwise and is certainly spiritually unsafe for human beings to persist in mating for life, particularly if there is any difference of opinion about what makes a joyful existence, if that's ever discussed at all. It wasn't in my case, though I know it was in yours. I'm not sure the way we've persisted with this sensible mating is natural. Maybe more like a habit and a nice illusion of security. But the truth is that with so much invested, there's more to lose.

My mother writes weekly to ask what is so terrible at home that I choose not to return to where everything is "so nice and peaceful." Maybe I'm too mad at my own country for not immediately intervening. Maybe I'm worried about being too near the old places, where there was so much damage done, although this is sometimes a frightening landscape—frankly, almost always. Despite the danger, despite the horrid sights and sounds beyond these windows, I never thought I would say that everything is a blessing, but it is. It would mean a great deal to me if you would write my mother and help her understand that I am here for the duration, bombs notwithstanding.

I fell asleep last night with my head on a man's chest, rising up and sinking down, evenly, rhythmically, but the sound explodes in each beat and moves out through my body in waves, and let me tell you I think I may have found my meaning of life in the sound of his heart, his breath, the rising up and sinking down. Other people can find theirs anywhere they please, but mine is here. We eat, drink, talk, make love, sleep, and when I believe I should leave, I do. Sometimes with tears. Sometimes not. But always glad and forever better for having known him, them.

Some know about the past in New York, as much as I felt comfortable telling, and others don't, and so we stay entirely in the present. I've learned that there's enough in the moment to talk about forever or until dawn, and it always amazes me. It isn't a game, and neither is it as flippant as moving from one to another lover. Part of losing one's mind after something so large as a marriage is destroyed comes of losing one's way in the world, but I have managed to find it instead. It started chiefly because of your family's insistence on truth, and then that mad affair I had at the Jefferson Hotel with the Hindu gentleman. And I thank you again for the key to your suite. I forgot to tell you, but you had done it up nicely. I loved the pleated linen bed skirt. The white brought it all together. Everything was bright and airy. Very needed. There was finally enough light to see into the days and the nights I might live and love through, not just breathe and take sustenance through.

He was the first man I may have ever loved the way it is intended, without the possession and the constant stress to please, to be perfect and pleasing, to be in a top mood all the time, even the once monthly when it's a struggle few of

us can win. Forever yanking on the ropes and pulleys behind the scenes of my married life fairly exhausted me, but
my husband enjoyed a wonderful show. Hard to believe
any man would be so stupid as to wrench such a charmed
life down on himself.

When you took me to Baltimore, the Hindu gentleman
didn't maneuver to go with me, and he didn't try to make
me stay. He encouraged me to leave. When this has happened, I find myself returning out of sheer desire, not guilt
or obligation. You were right when you told me that want
is more sensual than need. Men will say we cry and hang
on, looking desperate, and it's the last thing that makes
them want to stay, the first thing that drives them to someone else. Funny, but I don't remember ever doing that with
my husband, not ever. He was the one who was overheard
moaning about not knowing how he would live without
his "gem." Then, during the divorce, he told me that, unlike me, these whores would do anything to him that he
wanted. I thanked him for that image and said what
turned out to be the last words I ever spoke to him.

I told him, "Well, when you want those thick toenails
clipped, your ear hair trimmed, balm rubbed into that
scaly back, your Newport society friends placated, and so
forth, see how fast your whores get off their knees to do it.
And fine jewelry may look splendid on them naked in bed,
but you can't cover dirt in diamonds and take it to the
opera. If you're shameless enough to ever go there again,
and it'll be alone, you're going to realize what you lost the
minute you look toward those wide steps and don't see

me walking down them. And then if you go home and do away with yourself, see if any whore will clean up the mess. I'm through with it."

That was then. Now I have these days and nights of strong, luxurious love, and it feels and smells and tastes like raw perfection. Martha, I did not know I had a body. Neither did I know what it was willing to receive and willing also to do. It isn't the same as what he said about the women who'd do anything. I think he was referring to the elasticity of their limbs, not the bounty of their spirits.

When I was with a man who undressed me, picked me up and laid me down about two days later, I realized that my husband had done me a favor by underestimating how long I would be at the dentist's. When I found him with that girl, what they were doing was a sick and trifling approximation of what would've accomplished the same trick and been far less expensive to him had he simply taken care of it by himself. Now I can see that I walked in and caught a man in the act of dying. His mother has not stopped writing to me, wanting to know what I did to provoke him into infidelity. Let me tell you that I've decided that what men do to their mothers while calling out their wives' names is much more of an assault against ethics and morality than anything I've done in Paris.

Not too long ago, the brightest and most beautiful man I have ever known looked up at me and said he appreciated my weight on him when he was going off to sleep. Just the weight, Martha. The light heaviness of muscle and bone. I had a sense of a body. This good thing that I have and am was being loved hard. All my adult life, I've heard my "figure" praised. It was as though I was accepting the compliments on some other body's behalf, but now I'm wholly inside it, on my own ground, real, wet, dry, hot, cold, vibrating, and still.

I allowed you to assume that those days at the Jefferson were the first and last episodes of a cathartic fling. The truth of my silence is that I wanted to go a little longer and make sure that I hadn't made a horrible mistake before I disclosed it all to you. I couldn't announce a plan for my life and let you witness failure.

You wait with wisdom and act with assurance. I kept thinking of the way you trusted that you were making the best decision by not telling Mary about being in love again and having taken the suite at the Jefferson to be with him when he was in Washington. You said you would honor your child and keep that part of yourself to yourself, and then you went home and put that into action and did not back away or weaken. You told me, "I have a child who loves and misses her father. She does not deserve a mother whose heart is disjointed, waiting to see anyone else but her. She deserves both my eyes and my ears open. She did not ask for a pining, lovesick girlie for a mother."

You wanted love again because you'd been blessed with Grammar's, and it wasn't a trifling thing to have to learn to do without. But I wanted what I'd dreamed of and heard about from you since the day you saw him cutting up that old man's food when he was doing that work for St. Bart's, above the Beautiful Dreamer salon. Remember?

What impressed me more than anything is that Grammar never told you how you were supposed to be. But I chose someone who thought that I required constant direction. Remember when I couldn't tell you if I liked dark turkey meat? I don't know whether I had forgotten or was simply afraid to say.

When I booked the first ocean passage alone, I took what accommodation they wanted to give me, and paid an exorbitant fee, all because I'd become so bound up by the agent's questions. Which deck did I prefer? Did I want to engage the services of a porter? Did I want to pre-order a menu? I gave the agent the dates, told him to handle everything else, and got out of there as quickly as I could. He thought I was the type of person who couldn't be bothered by details, but the truth was that it was shaming to be indecisive because I had spent so many years giving over everything and myself. But I did sail the ocean like a queen.

I had to develop authority over myself. I had to see whether I could be in charge, from the largest notions of how I wanted to be to the smallest considerations of a day. All of which is to say I have done it, and am doing it, and I will be irritated if you become anxious for me in retrospect, about me drowning. There wasn't ever any danger.

Which brings me to what I wanted to say about a decision I think you should possibly consider making. Mary is such a kind and intelligent girl. Don't you think she's now grown-up enough to hear the news that her beautiful and responsible adult mother has a lover?

It is not as though you've kept him hidden because he's a drifter or a confidence man or someone who is seeking any kind of advantage, and it is not as though he is married. He's a brilliant, successful, well-regarded man who is devoted to you, and I'm sure she would love knowing him and would find so many things to admire. I've often wondered how you can sit beside her at a moving picture he made and not tell her anything. I would be up on the seat, shouting out loud that the man who created this picture loves me.

I agree that she should never know that you have turned down his proposals because you want her to feel a wholeness in your attentions. Of course, I don't have a child, but I think you're right to feel that she doesn't deserve the guilt. If she asks about why you haven't married him, you could lay the reason to his extensive travels, or you could simply say you don't want to, which is an entirely plausible thing to say, as you have never had that much difficulty with acting on your own counsel before.

But it is inarguable—you have given Mary a good life. She will want you to have yours without slipping out to do it. You know that the family across the street would agree. They have, after all, helped you keep this secret, taking her on trips with them, keeping her when he blew through Washington in a hurry. You've surrounded yourself with people who wish you only well, and she will continue to. It's in her nature, Martha. She is your child.

You need to remember this—that if you feel what you've done is immoral, then it was only because the im-

petus was to protect her, and in that universe of your family's, things like that have a way of canceling each other. Also, it is because you denied yourself and spent the time with her that she is now the type of young lady who would want only the best for you. You've raised her to have an open mind and a good heart, and if anyone should now reap some of the benefits of your efforts, it is you. She and I will both thank you for forever showing us the joy at the confluence of love and freedom.

My most dear portion,

Judith

Ten

Maureen read the last two paragraphs of Mrs. Stafford's letter again when she awakened the next morning. She then told me, "I fell asleep praying you weren't going to read a postscript that said, 'My husband eventually found me and dragged me home. All this joy for nothing.' As long as you don't say that, please tell me how it turns out at the very end. I'll go and do when I know."

"So far," I said, "she's still fine, still over there."

"And she's safe?"

"The last time she wrote to my mother, she told her she still felt safer than she had at home, even with the war. There's a great deal to be said for that."

Maureen spoke softly. "Yes, it was that way in Mississippi."

Mamie had brought her some bird's-eye that needed to be hemmed for diapers. Neither saw this as a violation of the prohibition. As Maureen pinned and stitched, I asked whether she had thought about making her own clothes again.

"Yes," she said, "all the time. They were always good, very good. He wouldn't have known they were homemade if he hadn't seen me at the machine. It took a woman with a good eye to detect the difference. I've sewn all my life. My father attached a block to the treadle so I could reach it."

"When my mother met you, you were in an extraordinary dress. She thought you'd made it, but that's not an insult. She has a good eye."

"I did make it, and I was so frightened of having the pattern drawn and then cutting in one inch too far at the end, wasting everything. "

"And you were wearing stockings with a vine around the ankles."

"Yes, I was," she said. "Let me ask you something. I want to know if your mother told Troop I looked cheap in them. I threw them away because he said she had."

"Maureen, she would never have said anything like that. The woman who sent those letters for you to read wouldn't have done it."

"Damn," she sighed, "they were the kind of hosiery that you mourn when they rip."

Maureen's aunt Stella ran the post office in Yazoo City. Part of that day's going and doing involved contacting the operator to put the call through, which required a balance of luck and skill that we were not too hopeful would work. But the effort gave Maureen some sense of control. I urged her to walk downtown and send a telegram, but she was reluctant for either of us to expose ourselves to whatever flu type of illness was circulating widely enough to be receiving coverage in the newspaper. Three people in Elm City had actually died with it one recent week. Maureen's doctor had missed his regular appointment with her the day before, and when I telephoned his office and said I could bring her there instead, the nurse told me that unless Maureen was sick herself, she should stay at home.

After we had called the operator, Mamie came into the room, her face strained with worry. Zollie's sister had sent word that one of the children was ill. "But," Mamie said, "Mr. Ross is at home for lunch today, and he said we were not bringing germs back in here, and if we leave, we leave for good."

Maureen hauled herself up and said, "No, you go. He can't say that."

"Well," Mamie said, "he has."

"You and Zollie both go home. Send somebody back to let me know what you need. Come back when you can. Mary, could you please go with her downstairs and help her get organized?"

Troop was there. In his presence, I told Mamie to have Zollie bring the car around so they would lose no time getting home. She would not look at Troop. She looked at her feet and left.

He said, "Are we giving away automobiles now?"

"Yes," I answered, "not to be overly dramatic, but there's something dangerous going around, and they have a child sick. The woman looking after the children isn't very competent, so they need to leave."

"They need to finish work," he said. He did not seem to notice that he might be drawing an indelible circle around himself. His wife and her mother were standing with Mamie and her children on the other side of the line.

"I can wash your dishes," I told him. "I can drive you to work in the other car. I can go back and pick you up and brush your clothes a thousand and one times tonight and then do it all again in the morning."

"I truly do not care," he said. "What you need to comprehend is that Mamie and Zollie will not come back to my home."

"Fine," I said, "I can handle everything." Knowing that the only thing more horrifying to him than having another person witness the goings-on of his household would be the vision of me sweeping leaves from the driveway, cleaning the front door, toting a basket to and from the market, I told him that I had done these chores all my life and was more than capable. "You have a perfectly strong and able-bodied poor relation ready to help," I said, "and I'm sure the neighbors have been wondering what I've been doing to earn my keep around here, besides feeding nerve pills to Maureen. You could hire someone else, but finding someone who won't take advantage, talk family business, or shed germs could take some investigating. So in the meantime, I can do everything."

"You think you're clever, don't you?"

"Yes, but not a miracle worker. Maureen and I have an operator trying to place a call to Mississippi, but I thought we might have better luck if you did it from your office. Would you be willing to do that?"

"Why do you need to call Mississippi?"

"Because Maureen needs to find out if her mother's alive."

He was becoming extremely edgy. He looked out the window. "Has something happened to her?"

"It's hard to say. You've been mailing Maureen's letters, and I assume that her mother has been writing to her in care of your office. But it's as though she died and nobody thought to tell Maureen."

"Yes," he said, "that's how those people are, uncouth and unreliable. The other postman we had here was just as unreliable. But who is it she needs to call down there? Her mother doesn't have a telephone."

"No, she doesn't. It doesn't sound like she has much of anything."

"Yes, it's a very unfortunate situation. And it's impossible to reach her by phone. It can't be done."

"Well, actually, it can. Maureen's aunt runs the post office in Yazoo City. The call gets made to her, and she takes things from there. So, you can place it?"

"I fail to see the sudden urgency, this frenzy."

"No frenzy," I told him. "Do I sound frenetic?"

"Something's behind this."

"Just imagine if you didn't know whether your mother was dead or alive, if you'd been mailing her letters with no response for a long time, if you'd told her about the baby and heard nothing."

"Yes, but this isn't anything that would ever be a concern. My mother was responsible and kept up with her correspondence."

"You certainly could say that."

"That wasn't an invitation to attack my mother's memory. The people who deserve the criticism are Maureen's. Those people she worships are so common that they do not comprehend standard behavior that people like you and me take for granted."

"So," I said, "you haven't seen any letters from Maureen's mother come to your office at all."

"No." He distracted himself with the business of getting back out of the house. "Not one. They should treat my wife better."

"I know. Fifty-seven dollars goes to them, and they shamelessly eliminate her from their lives."

"Yes," he said. "I need to go back to the office. We can talk about this another time."

"Do you want me to drive you?"

"No. It's a nice day out. I'll walk."

"Be careful of who you talk to on the way," I said. "You may want to put your handkerchief over your mouth. This flu, or whatever they're calling it now, is spreading everywhere, and it sounds terrible."

He told me he would be fine, and then left, still marvelously in control, but shaken and, I hoped, soon to fall.

Maureen and I waited an hour before she called his office

and asked for his secretary, who told her that she had heard nothing about a call to Mississippi. Maureen put her hand over the speaker and whispered to me, "What now? The letters?" I nodded.

"One more thing," she said to the secretary. "I'm working up a sort of surprise for my husband, and I would very much appreciate it if you would collect the letters that've come from Mississippi, addressed to me in care of him, all of them, and hold on to them until a young lady, Miss Oliver, comes over to pick them up later today." She listened and answered, "Yes, the telegrams as well. Thank you, and remember that this is part of a surprise."

She asked me how she sounded, and when I told her that the acting was much better than anything I'd seen involving the roses, she said, "That would be because this is real."

I asked if there was anything I could do before I went to Troop's office. "Yes," she told me. "Take every rose out of this house, and call the florist and tell him that any more deliveries will be turned away. I'm also going to give you a check to take to the bank to get a postal order and send it to my mother right away. And on that line for a note, write, 'Alive and flourishing. You were right.'"

After I did the things she needed, after getting in and out of my uncle's office without being seen by him, I took the box of letters to Maureen, all neatly arranged by date, all previously opened. "Well," she said, "I have something to pass the time between now and when the baby comes. This should keep the nervousness down, or at least replace one agitation with another. What was going through his mind when he was reading them and then keeping them away like this?"

I told her that I had no idea but I was sorry. She asked to be left alone to read, and assured me that she would call me if she needed me. Within minutes, she was at the top of the steps, calling me back. She was holding one of the letters, astounded. "You have to hear this, Mary. I started reading them backward."

September 30, 1918
Dear Maureen,

Just a note first of all to say I hope that you are well and although part of me wonders if you are dead or simply have DECIDED TO HATE ME, I LOVE YOU all the same. And if what I think is going on is actually going on, I am even more worried than I thought I was. But before I say what I need to about your husband, I intend to write EVERYTHING that is on my mind.

I try not to say anything to interfere with people. Maureen, you're grown and can do what you want. But we were talking and talking through the mail and then NOTH-ING. I thought that telegrams had to get there by law, and I've sent them and I'm getting concerned that you are so silent.

If I said something that stung, I can make it up to you. But I don't think it's that. When you lived at home, if we had a hard word, we straightened things out. I remember you used to tell me that it made you afraid to go to bed with worry in you. There isn't anything you could do to make me stop loving you, so NEVER BE WORRIED about that.

If you have a problem with some way you were raised, you can say it. I wasn't able to get you things out of the picture magazines, but you had everything you needed. You always acted happy when I got some nice fabric and we sat down and copied the dresses from the pictures, but if you get mad about that when you wear your things from the store now, I understand how it'd make you feel. I just did not think that I had raised a child who would act like she was happy and loved her family when she was simply HIDING SPITE. I am here to tell you that that is the WRONG way to live.

Call me lazy and say you wish I'd worked harder if you need to. I know there were days I could've gotten to work before 6, but you and a sister or two would have those long legs thrown over me, sleeping with your mouths open, drooling, laughing in your sleep, and I'd ask myself if leaving you was worth the extra dollar. The way you felt was always worth more. If I made the wrong decision, I just have to say I'M SORRY.

But I know in my heart that you are not that kind of young lady. That has just been on my mind lately. What I really think is YOUR HUSBAND DOES NOT TREAT YOU RIGHT. Sometimes I wonder if he has stopped treating you like a HUMAN BEING. He isn't the kind of man that ties you up and sits over in the corner, watching you starve to death. He lacks the nerve and patience. He's the kind that ties you up and then goes and eats a tenderloin steak and then comes in and forgets to check on you before he goes to sleep for the night.

I read about a man in Jackson who did that to his mother. She had turned into a bag-o-bones by the time they found her, and the son was off on a Cuban vacation. They said he gave out cigars to the police. You and I both know that your husband is cut from that same bolt of cloth. You know it, but you try to forget on account of the sheer embarrassment that you got duped. You may not want to admit that you married somebody WHO DOES NOT WISH YOU WELL. But I am your mother. I do not want to blame you and will not. I want you safe and free from worry, which is the true meaning of heaven on earth.

I wish I'd stopped the marriage from happening to begin with. BUT I DIDN'T. Everybody in Mississippi had a funny feeling long before the wedding. Then, after you did not come home when Ella and Eloise died, all I heard was how this isn't Maureen making this decision and she is not a girl who would ignore her family and act like her sisters burning to death in a fire was none of her concern. Everybody in Mississippi said they bet that Maureen was up in N.C. being ground completely down to where she no longer knows her own mind, or is afraid to speak it. We all knew he was made entirely of lies, Maureen. We should've gone up there and GOTTEN YOU OUT. Because GETTING OUT is what you will have to do if what I believe is true.

YOU CANNOT REPAIR OR CHANGE A PERSON LIKE HIM on account of he will tell you there isn't anything wrong with him and call you the crazy one for thinking it. The only way to live with people like him in this world is to stay as far away from them as possible. Those who were at the wedding said how Troop was so full of flattery and how he wouldn't go to all that trouble to behave like somebody he wasn't unless he was straining to keep the nobody he actually was out of sight. You can't fool Mississippi.

Remember when he visited our house and WOULD NOT DRINK THE WATER you had pumped from the well? He wouldn't wash his hands in it either. Then he poured out his glass and tried to show you there was something crawling on the bottom of it, I guess hookworms or something of that nature. I remember the way you looked at me and then him and then agreed with him. I tricked you into coming out to the yard with me, where I said you could expect that kind of belittlement the rest of your life. HE WAS A SNOB. Then he had the gall to pay Ella a dime to walk a mile to the store and buy him a root beer in a bottle although we had that here HOMEMADE as well. I hate to think of how many times since then he has held a clean glass at your face and made you say you see something that is not there. That is in a manner of speaking, but you understand.

I bet you that when your lives got out of the fairy tale stage, when you had to come out of the honeymoon cottage and carry out the real order of your days, that Troop started not to get his way all the time. NOBODY DOES IN THIS LIFE. After a while, a woman looks around and sees that there is more pressing business than flattering a man and dolling up for him all the time. And that is when you had better genuinely like and appreciate the other person the way you do a brother or sister or your oldest friend, or everything they do will grate on you so badly you will want to cut your own throat and wash the blood down with poison to escape another hour with them.

And there is yourself to care for, Maureen. You always liked who you were inside. Your husband seems to be a person who is sick in love with himself. He is the kind that has affairs so he can be constantly fed the news of what a champ he is. Troop did not like you, Maureen, not a bit. Not who you are, funny and good and wise and honest. And he hated us and our country ways and had a hard time appreciating the fact that a home that smells like smoke and supper all the time is not suffocating. IT IS LIFE. I raised you to be kind and do your best, and you are with a man who was raised to crave attention and get something for nothing. And he got you.

He liked the idea that somebody with a good heart like you cared about him, and I guarantee the first time you showed some dissatisfaction, it wasn't any turning back after that. If I didn't know all this, I'd be UNFIT to be your mother. I cannot imagine what all he has put in your head. But it needs to come out, if I need to send your uncles up there with an auger. Maybe what will happen is that he will push and push and you will take it and take it and then he will eventually do something that takes *your breath away. You cannot imagine how it HURTS me to say these things, but knowing that you're locked in that life with him hurts more. You will heal from your wounds. He won't. BUT I DO NOT CARE.*

Maureen, I want you to listen when I say that although you may choose not to talk to your mother or sisters that you must talk to somebody. You have to find somebody to talk to immediately who is not fooled by him. But be careful of what you tell those society doctors on account of if you say you are UNHAPPY they will want to RIP YOUR FEMALES out. They are not what give you light and life, but if they are taken out against your will the way they did my friend down here, then you will have a hole in yourself and also be off the monthly custom. It is one thing for nature to leave you naturally but another to have your body CUT OPEN AND ROBBED because a man wants you to shut up at supper.

If it was me, I would set the bastard up and be out of there so fast that the wind at my back knocked him down. If you would write, I could help you. But I cannot think that you have gone over to his ways and that I now have a ZOMBIE DAUGHTER. And I hate to say this, but be careful about having a baby, unless you already have. Think if you want to be tied to that man the rest of your life.

The minute I was told to send things in care of Troop, I knew the story. But even the way he treated you at the dinner table here was ENOUGH. The thought of any of my girls living in a house where they are made to be afraid is intolerable. There is no way for me to ask you to let me know if you are not getting mail from me. Is there, Troop?

Troop, are you listening? What kind of pleasure are you taking from watching my girl suffer? You have caused Mississippi a great deal of turmoil and frustration but the mills of the Gods are going to eventually grind you up and spit you out. And there won't be a soul left to watch. So you'll be lacking in that little bit of personal attention as well.

I'm out of this tablet of paper. But that was about all anyway, except I still love my girl,

Mama

The love and honor of her mother's words must've shaken him to the core. And there were other letters like this. I can't imagine him thinking that if he kept her mother's evaluation of his character away from her perhaps she would never know what she was involved in. All I could say when I finished reading was, "Aunt Maureen, I don't know what to say. But it certainly sounds like your mother doesn't want or need fifty-seven dollars, or any amount of salvation from the swamps. She wants her daughter."

"I know," Maureen replied. "When we were sitting at the table, staring into the glass, I looked straight at my mother and said, 'Yes, he's right. The glass may have some kind of worms at the bottom. Something's definitely in there.'"

"Did you love him that much? I know you thought you could use his money to improve your family's situation, but that's hardly grounds for marriage."

"You see, Mary, I could not believe that somebody with that much polish and sophistication would have anything to do with me. The boy I took company with in Yazoo City became the most successful hog farmer in the state, but he was lacking in class. He didn't know how to act in public. He didn't know how to hold himself. Troop smiled and was so at ease in situations I wasn't comfortable in that I felt guided along. I was gliding in a world I thought I'd never enter. But now I see that he was only comfortable with people he thought were his social equal or better, and if we were at a party and I spoke to someone from the kitchen, he'd hold it against me for weeks, months. He's always thought everybody was looking at him and making judgments, and then I started bringing down their opinion of him. His mother was so critical of him, although you'd never hear him say it. But I knew. I had this sense of him growing up choking and desperate for her to show him some true, motherly affection.

"Maureen, it seems to me that he was afraid of making her angry and jealous, but as far as I know, and it isn't that much, men don't draw their love for their wives and their love for their mothers from the same well."

"I've always heard that, and even common sense tells you it's a different kind of love. But when I told him that, he glared at me until I thought his face was going to explode, and he said I was perverted, a bitch."

I asked Maureen what she was going to do now.

"I'm going to put this letter on his pillow and let him sleep on it tonight," she replied, "and then we'll see what happens in the morning. Maybe he'll call me a bitch again. And I'm going to think what to do about Mamie and Zollie. That's enough for today. It's more than I generally do in a year."

"Have you ever thought of leaving, going back home?"

"All the time, yes, but then I think of what it would be like to be alone, and I stop."

"Maureen, you're already alone. Don't you see that?"

"Mamie and Zollie are here."

"He may not let them come back."

"I'm going to have a baby," she said. "There'll be love here soon. Everything will be fine on the other side of Thanksgiving."

Eleven

He said nothing about the letter she left on his pillow, but he walked around the two of us in wide circles that grew wider and wider—so wide that, three days later, I found a note on the kitchen table informing that he was gone to Durham on business for a few days. She was so certain that he would find retribution irresistible that she curled herself in bed, closed her eyes, and waited. Over the years, she told me, she had called this time the eye of the tornado. She knew to be as still as possible and to stay mindful and respectful of what was coming.

When I told her that we may have diverted the storm by letting him know she was no longer ignorant, she said, "No.

I don't think so. Every waking thought he has is about avoiding humiliation. He can control anything for any amount of time, so long as he does not have to feel embarrassment. The Second Coming won't catch him off guard."

"Do you think he'll change at all when the baby comes?" I thought I knew the answer, but mine wasn't the one that mattered.

"Yes, I've been asking myself what kind of life this child is going to have if she has to watch me crawl from one day to the next."

"Then you're sure the baby is a girl?"

"Never tell anybody I said this, but if it's a boy, I'll be scared of him, terrified actually. Troop wouldn't be as concerned with a girl, but he would make a boy just like himself. He would *take* him. I mean, he wouldn't teach a boy right from wrong. He wasn't taught. My mother knew the difference between discipline and punishment, but Troop cannot endure the simplest correction. Everything and everybody is against him, or that's what he thinks. A girl doesn't believe that as readily. Anyone who doubts it should check into an asylum and listen to how complaints vary between the males and the females there. You see, when I went to the hospital for those hysteria treatments, I had to stay for weeks, and it was the men who screamed that the deck was stacked against them or that people were out to get them or were lined up against them.

"It was purely imaginary, but even if it hadn't been, I wanted to scream back, 'Well, you're big enough, and stronger than we are, with a thousand years of advantages, so get up and do something about it.' But the women, most of them were like me, committed by their husbands. They all knew beyond the absolute shadow of a doubt that somebody was out to get them. It was real. So many of them were told repeatedly that their children were going to be taken away if they didn't improve. And if the women did act odd, if they sat in a corner and rocked, if they cried continuously, it looked to me like they had just been pushed past the walls of their endurance. They had something to cry and chew their hands and bang their heads on the wall about. And they didn't blame everybody else for their problems. Whether they deserved it or not, they blamed themselves. But as black as their moods were, there was quick, a spark of life, you know, somewhere inside. It was there, even if they were the only ones who believed it."

"Then how did you know it was there?" I asked.

"Because we weren't dead yet. We had not decided to be dead. The doctors thought that happiness could be shocked back into us. They put one very sweet and depressed lady through the horror of having a man wearing a ghoul mask sent into her room at night, after they had doped her up with chloral hydrate. He stood by her bed with a candle and shouted her awake, frightening her out of her wits. And the next day, when she was still without any reason at all, they decided it might work better if they had her husband come in and tell her that her children had died. I still thank God they decided that shocking my system with buckets of ice and electrical current was enough for me. But I don't know. What Troop has done, hiding my old life from me, is just a slow, dawdling form of shock torture. What I couldn't say, because he was always, always at my meetings with the doctors, was that as long as they were doing these things to me and then sending me home with him, nothing was ever going to change. We rode the train home from the hospital, and he rode me the entire distance, examining me about what nasty things I had told the nurses about him, accusing me of twisting his words and doing unspeakable things with the orderlies. I could hardly walk into the house."

"Why did you stay?" I asked.

"My family had stopped communicating with me. Where was I going to go? I decided to try out for school, to take some courses at the women's college here. And during one of those times, about ten months ago, when Troop was being decent, I told him about the plans. I thought he'd be thrilled that I wanted to better myself. He has so many difficulties with things like my accent. But he called the doctor, and the next week I heard about the surgery."

"Maureen, he was afraid you were going to leave."

"No, I wasn't going to. I just wanted something for myself."

"It's the same thing to him."

I understood better, after she told me these things, why she was lying so still, waiting for what she knew would inevitably hit. But what neither Maureen nor her husband knew, and what I felt when I pressed my hands against her silk-covered womb, was that she had the power of God in her now, and the will of her mother, two certainties that would protect and honor her with such force of love that they were eternal and irrevocable, never at a man's mercy again.

A storm was starting to blow outside, but we were able to hear the bell toll three times in succession. That morning, a letter from home had assured me everyone in Washington was well, but Mother said that things around the government buildings were a little strange. Our neighbor's son worked for the Department of the Navy, and he told her that everybody in the building was issued a surgical mask and made to go outside several times a day for fresh air. Billy Sunday had said that the flu was God's vengeance for the depravity of modern life and could be prayed away. An editorial had noted that butchers and Methodists were not coming down with it. After being with Maureen for these weeks, I didn't automatically dismiss any such ideas as senseless. I considered the scores of people who would read those words and take them at face value, good and decent people, not people who were too gullible and inane to function in society. My uncle had been able to convince doctors that his wife was insane, by describing reality in a way that supported his claim. But what he did not tell them was that the words he was using were as well chosen as everything else in his life, thus ensuring that he could keep her. Anyone, I decided, would believe anything, as it required nothing, and questioning was far too much trouble.

I am still amazed that my uncle was able to maintain his composure and charming affect, given the pressure he needed to exert constantly to hold his wife down. Presenting a false impression to his half sister was a simple matter of writing words on paper to someone hundreds of miles away. I could only wonder what sort of model husband and father he might be if he changed. But change that elemental would come only if he hit bottom, such an unpleasant place for him to regard that I knew he would never reach it. Opportunities had come and gone, and Maureen was no longer willing to sacrifice another day of her future or her child's to him, in anticipation of the day when he could admit that he was as human and vulnerable as the rest of us, no better, no worse.

He had squandered years of her life. He had courted and married a rigorous beauty whose spirit and nature proved antithetical to his; facing her day after day must have forced a reluctant and impossible self-examination and created in him an ear-ringing panic. A weak husband living with an excellent woman—that is enough to scare a man to death and shake him off his rails. And he had the shame of knowing that anything he truly loved about life, when all the pretense was put aside, had come from her. It wasn't his. She might have been temporarily lacking in some of the choicest parts of a soul—humor, curiosity, passion—but that was because her husband had resorted to this thievery of spirit to acquire them, to hoard them for himself or perhaps out of the conviction that she didn't deserve to have anything that she was weak enough to let him take. He had weakened her and then despised her inability to fight. But I was holding a woman who was resting now, conserving her energy, and sometime before Thanksgiving, when it was increased by the labor of birthing and then caring for the child, she would be far too busy to hear her husband's distress. And I believed he would be distressed, and he would let her know it. I imagined him standing alone on the inside of his own terror, pleading for her to push the baby aside and make room for him in her heart.

When he returned from Durham, he came to find us in her bedroom. I was in a corner, fixing the bobbin on her sewing machine. He stood at the foot of the bed and stared at her as she lay there, propped on pillows, resting. Her body was wet with an evening's perspiration, fecund, round, and whole. When he saw me, he started, sniffed the air, and said it was putrid. He wasn't able to admit that he was watching Venus. The Hindu levitationist would have called him a fool and then closed the door on him and raised Venus from her sleep. If her husband was ever due any pity, it was then.

He decided not to bother her and left. When Maureen awakened, I told her he was back.

"Then I need to put my mind elsewhere. I can see him roaming around, looking for things I've left out of place."

"I've been keeping things fairly decent in Mamie's absence," I told her.

"No, that's not what I mean. I mean, I can see him looking for any reason to correct me. You need to distract me from this. Just talk. Tell me something good. Tell me about your parents."

I told her how they had met during my father's last semester in New York, when he was earning his school expenses by delivering pastoral care for St. Bart's. My mother was busy avoiding everything Barnard had to offer in favor of strolling around New York, looking extremely pretty, forever with Judith Benedict on one arm and a department store parcel on the other. The two of them had a standing appointment with a woman who interpreted dreams and manicured nails simultaneously in a tiny shop called Beautiful Dreamer. It was located on the ground floor of the tenement where Father did most of his work. After they courted for as long as my mother's patience would allow, she withdrew from Barnard and married my father at St. Bart's, on a sweltering July afternoon. She loved describing how twenty-five spiffy derelicts in matching straw boaters supplied by my father, along with a cluster of literature professors, young ministers, milliners, seamstresses, hairdressers, manicurists, palm readers, astrologists, and various other prophets filled the pews and mixed admirably at the reception.

"It doesn't seem real," Maureen said.

"I'm not sure," I replied, "but it seems more real than this."

"Tell me, did your mother follow Judith's advice? Did she ever say anything about the man at the hotel?"

"No, nothing was ever said of it. I liked to believe that one day I would happen to be at the hotel having dinner with friends and she and I would see each other. And then she would pass me and step into the elevator. She deserves to believe she protected me, because she did. And your mother did the same. She stayed in bed with you instead of going to work for that extra dollar. She didn't parade men through the door after your father died."

Maureen closed her eyes for a few minutes and then

spoke. "I think I can face Troop now. Do you mind asking him to come in here?"

I found him at his desk. Though he pestered me about why he was being summoned, he followed me upstairs. She was waiting, sitting beautifully erect, smiling.

Her voice was even. "I want you to tell me about the letters."

"Maureen, I don't know what you're doing digging into my personal affairs, but I didn't give you the letters because I didn't want to upset you. I suppose I get no credit for that. And if I had sent your mother all the things you wrote, all the private things about my home, it would've constituted an even more egregious invasion of my privacy."

"Listen to yourself. Not a word you said was true. Not a thing. Surely you can't believe that learning my baby sister won a beauty contest would tip me over the edge. That knowing my uncle was named head deacon would make me slit my wrist? That hearing my mother's garden was coming in would make me take an overdose? That the fact everybody seemed to be getting past their grief would somehow upset me? Is any of that disturbing? Don't answer. You're incapable of telling the truth if a lie would hurt me. But why did you bother to save them? I know you read them. But why save them? Did you keep them to torture yourself? Or to have the thrill of knowing that I was going without them? You accuse me of invading your privacy. Those words, Troop, were not yours to take or to keep. You may as well have walked in on my mother and me sitting here talking and slapped both of us in the mouth. And you're a man. Are you ever going to stop behaving like a spoiled, jealous child?"

"Maureen," he said sharply, "you're thoroughly out of control. I'm not obliged to answer you. But I'll say this. I have a right to read anything that comes out of this house, be it your whining or your lying. You are my wife, no matter what Mata Hari here has tried to do to undermine that. I see you two sleeping together. It disgusts me. How would your mother like to know that?" He tore open a box of stationery, snatched his pen out of his vest, and threw it and a flurry of paper across the bed. "Go ahead," he said, "write her. Do it. Do it now."

I came around the bed and stood in front of him. "Get out," I told him.

He wouldn't move. He glared at me, stabbing out the words: "She is going to be taken somewhere and kept until that baby is born."

"Good," I said, "I can have her on the next train to Washington."

He poked me in the chest with his finger. "I'll have the police on you before the train reaches Washington, and you'll be arrested and prosecuted for kidnapping."

Maureen was weeping, already despairing over winning any kind of battle with him, knowing he would never apologize or concede.

He strode across the room, and slammed the door behind him.

"Mary," she asked, "did I look or sound out of control?"

"No, you didn't. People are murdered for less than what he's done, what he does. You are not crazy, Maureen. But I'm not feeling too rational right now myself. And you've been taking this for how many years?"

"Forever," she said, "and it's not over yet."

I pulled the thick hair from her neck and wound it around in my hand, and I sat there looking at her, wondering whether I shouldn't get her on the next train. Maybe the time had come to leave. Yet when I told her this, she said, "I can't. Please, no more. I can't."

When she had gathered herself, she said, "I've figured it out, just now, while I was lying here."

She had made a decision, not about what to do next, but about her past.

"I asked myself why I let myself be with someone like him. You see, I've never read a romance. I always thought them silly, and I've resented the expectation, when I telephone the bookseller, that I'm going to order a bundle of them. I've not read one, but I know they all feature women who love the wrong man, soften the hearts of beasts, and without fail, everything turns out to the heroine's advantage. Maybe that kind of lunatic optimism is something we pick up along the way, whether we read those books or not. Somehow we all get notified that life is supposed to be like that."

"So Maureen, where did your 'lunatic optimism' come from?"

"It certainly wasn't from my mother."

"Mine, either."

"What did she say you were supposed to do instead?"

"Make your bed," I told her. "She said a woman is supposed

to get up and make her bed and then make the rest of the day up the best way she can. I think she intended me to find romance in that."

"Did you?"

"I believe I have."

"Do you think my mother would bring her rifle up here?"

"Yes. And my mother would meet her in your front yard, and what Troop calls a 'scene' would play out in front of everybody. You could guess who would be left standing at the end of that novel."

"Yes," she said. "That's one I think I could tolerate."

Twelve

Before I had departed Washington in September, I visited my academic advisor at her home. I had told her where I was about to go and some of the reason, and as I was leaving, she said, "Make good use of these months, Mary. Women like us aren't given time."

She was such a serious person, always available to prove her worth and her value. Sometimes I wanted her to stop pressing me to do the same. I had no desire to carry myself for the next fifty years, whether anyone was noticing or not, as an example that a woman could study, learn, and teach as well as a man. I didn't want to leave with that fatalistic advice at my back, so I turned to her, laughing, and asked, "Well, what are women like us given?"

"Nothing, Miss Oliver, not a damn thing." Then she smiled and wished me a safe journey.

Now, after another couple of days passed with my uncle's silent hostility, I was fearful of driving to Mamie's house and finding sickness or death, terrified I'd bring it back and kill Maureen and the baby, so I did nothing. Yet there was no word from Mamie. The cold snapped the leaves off the trees outside the tall windows, and the expected declaration of an end to the fighting overseas dragged from one day to the next.

The bells continued their tolling, and people in the streets were now wearing masks. Terror that the baby would become sick and die inside her blistered Maureen's nerves so badly that she took as fact the milkman's rumor that the Germans had somehow broken into our atmosphere and poisoned our air. "I know I'm being unreasonable," she told me. "The Germans are just a misguided group of people. But this is too evil to be random, and during a war. Things don't happen like this, not this much sickness and death."

Mother and I had made several attempts to talk, but she had quarantined herself with my grandparents, and Grandmother Leslie, who feared that germs came through the telephone, would grab the earpiece and slam it down when she caught someone on the telephone. Mother had been able to tell me that the house was backlogged with arriving ghosts: "Mary, anyone who's ever doubted the ghosts in the walls should be here," she said. "It's like Union Station on Friday afternoon, everybody mad about the lines and the wait. Until I was surrounded by this much death, I don't think I appreciated how thick it can be in a house so full of spirits. The dead are grieving the dead. But the good news is that they're not as self-centered as they used to be." And then there was a commotion, and my grandmother's shouts of "The two of you are going to die on the long-distance telephone. Hang it up now!" and the connection was broken.

Later I received a letter from Mother by special post. The week before, her father had tripped over a branch in the backyard and then lain there insensible for hours, until Grandfather Leonard discovered him. Although nothing was determined broken, the fall had injured his confidence and his sense of authority. The doctor he trusted was away with the army in France, and the new man who examined him all but called him a crackpot and questioned the sanity of any method of life that would lead a man to be found naked in his yard in the middle of a weekday afternoon. The doctor had recognized him from a newspaper profile that had run a few weeks previously. Mother enclosed the clipping, in which Grandfather Toby had quite heartily admitted, "I was loathed by my first wife and my son for having mortified them with what she took to be a few tendencies toward recidivism in the area of moral turpitude, but I have always loved nature and like to be as close to it as possible. I thrive on the cool open air, blowing across all my human being."

Mother wrote, "He could've accepted being called eccentric. He's accustomed to it. But he could not bear the implication that his life was naively misspent or that he'd grown feeble-minded. When we got home from the doctor's and told the others what he had said, they sent the doctor a pair of game hens with a note—'We hope this plump set of chickens covers the crackpot's bill.' Father now refuses to consult any doctor besides the dead and alcoholic one who lives behind his bedroom wall. He resists rest but is mending nonetheless. At least it is not the flu. There have been daily notices in the paper for doctors who remember 'even a little' of their profession to come out of retirement and ease the shortage, so perhaps a dead drunkard is not so bad."

Within days after I received that letter, she placed a call to tell me that the perky mother of five down the street had died. Days later, she placed another call, to tell me about one of my elementary school teachers who had died, and about our mailman's son, who had been in especially close quarters with the flu on what could have been a celebratory voyage home from the Western Front. You might have heard the uproar of a thousand men as the ship left the port at Brest, but it was deathly still when it reached America. He survived the front but did not last the return. The replacement mailman told Mother that the boy's father had gone to Baltimore and found enough of his son to satisfy him among other soldiers who had sickened and died so grievously and melted into one another. A sailor rushed the mailman and the other fathers because he wanted to get the deck scoured before dark.

Mother was weeping on the telephone, but she gathered herself. "Mary, that same doctor who saw your grandfather said more or less that nice people, you know, people of good association, apparently even the old kooks among them, probably won't be stricken as badly, because of nutrition and hygiene. I thought that was an incredibly snobbish thing to say." Then she asked timidly, "But do you think that might be true? Maybe?"

I could hardly criticize the snobbery, as I was reading the same thing, and I had started to tell myself that people like us were not the ones who suffered and died from this kind of spreading, fulminating disease. But when the newspaper began running a notice called "Prominent People Who Have Died of the Flu," listing their hometowns and achievements, I realized that if business and political leaders could die, if Wayland Trask, the Keystone actor, could die, and if the King of Spain could fall desperately ill, then nothing we owned amounted to enough of a defense. People in my aunt's neighborhood thought themselves immune because they could afford clean and spacious surroundings, ample food, daily baths, and ludicrous precautions like surgical and gas masks. The gadgets were soon left aside, mainly because they were inconvenient. One morning when I went to the street for the mail, a neighbor praised me for not stooping to wear a mask. "The one my husband brought home," she said, "made me look silly."

But for a couple of weeks masks were the rage, like pugs and Italian greyhounds, among people who wanted to show sympathy and support for the poorer classes. When several local philanthropists were interviewed, they emphasized that their hearts went out to the sections of town that were habitually marked for this kind of devastation, that those people were in their prayers, and that they had high hopes for their luck to improve. The couple across the street from Maureen did take enough pity on their servants to make them line gravy strainers with gauze and walk around with these pressed up to their faces. They must've had only three strainers, because two of the maids had to go about with their entire heads wound in mosquito meshing.

I thought the maids might know something of Mamie's sick child. One of them told me, "She's nursing her sons is all I know." I hadn't realized until then that both children were sick. Maureen gave me a note with some money for Mamie, and I brought it across the street, where one of the women agreed to deliver it. When I returned to the house, I walked straight into my uncle, who asked what I had been doing across the street. I told him about Mamie's sons.

"It's more likely they needed time off to attend that suspect colored revival set up by the train station. Maybe they were seized by the spirit or by whatever patent cure that crowd's selling. Or maybe they've just gone off in the woods for a few days. We know how that works, don't we?"

"And you know, Zollie prefaces everything with, 'I don't mean any disrespect,' but I think I do. You managed to slight so much in one statement, and you know nothing about any of it. And they're not having a revival in that tent by the depot, or selling patent medicine. They're selling coffins."

"I didn't ask for this information," he said. "But this is what I would like to know. You're going to be with us how much longer?"

"January."

"Then in January you'll be free to manage your life. Until then, I'll decide whether the help gets to keep setting their own schedule and also whether money is handed over to a negress, with a high unlikelihood of it reaching its destination."

I managed to say, "So you do not want me to pursue any way of getting help to them?"

"No, because they aren't coming back to this home. Let them find somebody else to dupe into financing their lives. I'm sending the sheriff out to get the automobile, and then I wash my hands of them."

"What are you going to do without them? What's Aunt Maureen going to do?"

"I can eat downtown. You're here. She'll be fine."

"She's having a baby in a few weeks."

"The doctor knows the way to the house. He'll be willing to come daily for any installments of her melodrama she would like to relate to him, all of which have only served thus far to make her appear more in need of help than she may actually be."

"No, I did not mean that the doctor is needed. I've been able to hold things together since Mamie had to leave, but Maureen needs more help than me, not only for herself but for this household. Surely you realize that. I simply cannot keep up anymore. This is too huge a place."

"I know you're used to having everything handed to you. Self-sufficiency must be a foreign notion, despite that ludicrous claim about doing your 'chores' in Washington. And

Maureen's gotten rather fond of having everybody jump when she snaps. She's exhausted everybody. If I'm not careful, she's going to deplete me as well. In fact, one thing that might have happened, which you don't seem very eager to credit, is that Mamie and Zollie couldn't tolerate it anymore and just left. Do you know how embarrassing it would be for you to go retrieve these people and find out that they were just waiting for a chance to leave?"

I heard and felt my heart beating in my neck. I didn't know whether he was lying or if he really saw the life around him that way. He wasn't displaying a liar's typical agitation. I'd studied literature and imagined the strangest things about strangers, and nothing was ever close to this. What I could say to him, what I felt indisputably safe to say was, "I'm sorry, but all I saw was kindness on both sides, Maureen's and theirs, all around."

"There's such a thing as seeing what you want to see. Maybe your grandfather's blind spot is a congenital defect you've inherited."

In a basket on the kitchen counter were two rolls, all that remained of those I'd bought earlier from the only market that hadn't been closed for the flu precaution. He picked them up and wrapped them in his handkerchief.

"I bought those for Aunt Maureen—to settle her nausea. She asked for something to soak up the acid in her stomach, and the doctor recommended unbuttered bread. He assured me this symptom was not associated with the flu."

Putting the rolls back in the basket, he said, "She's welcome to them. But she's only going to get sick again if she crams herself full of bread. Her stomach is upset, Mary, because she's having a baby. Do you want to provoke another cycle of calling the doctor for consolation?"

"No. I saw her vomiting. It happened three or four times yesterday. My mother says nausea is unusual this late in a pregnancy.

"I was wondering how long you could subsist without consulting Washington. I wonder, too, when you will learn that no amount of reassurance can satisfy Maureen."

"No amount? I haven't seen any."

He was about to speak, when Maureen appeared in the doorway. Her wrapper was undone, as she was too large for it to be any other way. She seemed not to have heard him, didn't even acknowledge his presence. She said nothing about being hungry, even though that must have been why she had come downstairs. She sat down at the table and opened the newspaper.

Troop could not ignore his compulsion to wound her, as bad as she looked and obviously felt. "Maureen," he said, "would you please advise your mascot to stop glaring at me?"

She said only, "I thought you had a meeting this morning."

"I thought I did, but I just realized that my schedule was given to me incorrectly."

He stood at the kitchen desk, going through mail and the past two or three days' newspapers while she and I sat at the table, reading. And then, as though nothing had happened, as though he were spending his morning with people who enjoyed his company and looked forward to what he had to say, he told us to listen. "This is phenomenal." He intended to read to us from the paper, and after he had, he brought it over and spread out the pages so we could read it for ourselves.

What had excited him was an advertisement on the obituary page for a particular model of casket called "Awake!" There was no price listed, but this model was meant to appeal to "those who would cherish hope" and those who know that "the mortician is only human"—that he could have misdiagnosed a coma or, given the huge number of flu victims coming through his door, in his rush skipped over a customer entirely. Anyone who opened his eyes and found himself unlucky enough to have been buried alive better have been lucky enough to have been laid out in the Awake! With the aid of the long rubber voice-and-oxygen tube and the tins of rations, anyone who was not utterly terrified to death could eat and scream until he was rescued.

A survivor would have had to be extremely well-off, incredibly distrustful, and heady with some order of that lunatic optimism to make this purchase. And while there would be nothing remotely tasteful about a funeral or wake that featured the thing, my uncle, after scrutinizing the finest print with great care, telephoned the undertaking concern and left an urgent message that he be sent the exact specifications. He had one of these in mind for himself, he said, for if his death resulted from this flu, he wanted Maureen to question the pronouncement immediately, have him checked and double-checked, and just to be on the safe side, install him in one of the contraptions. Money, he said, was no object, and she was to waste no time in spending it on him.

Aunt Maureen had her head in her hands. She did not ask, but I did. "Have you lost your mind?"

"Certainly not," he said.

"Then I suppose Aunt Maureen can also count on an Awake!" I said.

"Of course she can. What kind of question is that?"

What else was he going to say? That he planned to dig a hole and throw her in it? After she'd been silent for too long to suit him, he asked whether she was going to thank him. So she did. She lifted her head, looked directly at him, and in the most detailed way conceivable, thanked him profusely for rescuing her from the grave. She went as far as to thank him ahead of time for being thoughtful enough to pack her with her favorite tinned potted meats and peaches. Instead of gratitude for the roses, it was gratitude for her own grave. If this scene had been taking place at the breakfast table of any other couple in the world, they would've been laughing at the absurdity of the thing. But he wasn't laughing, and neither was she.

"It'll be grand," she went on to say, "to have somewhere so comfortable to be, everything so well thought out, everything so handy there to eat. The more I think about it, the more appealing it sounds. Troop, maybe you do intend to take care of me. Maybe I've been worried about nothing."

Even he was impressed. Her remarks were much more credible than those about the roses. Either she had become a professional-grade liar or she had finally gone mad, and it didn't matter to him—he actually indicated his pleasure at the arrival of this moment by nodding and winking at me, as though I were suddenly complicit and just as glad as he.

Without changing her tone, she continued: "But what about the rolls? Can you make sure someone puts them in the coffin in case I feel as pukish as I do right now? I heard you just before I came in, Troop, and since you know everything about me, perhaps you can tell me who gave you the power to know when I'm sick and when I'm well? How far can you take this? Do you intend to tell the undertaker that I've faked my own death to get attention? Would you tell people I had myself buried alive to make you pity me? You know what, Troop? I don't need you, but I need attention. I am having a baby. I need attention. That's what married people give each other. I'm not trying to snatch anything from you, but I deserve something beyond what I'm getting right now. I admit it. I want to be with a kind, honest human being. There."

He smiled. "Such high drama, Maureen. People have babies every day, every minute of the day. Why is this experience any different from any other?"

"Because it's yours. That's why it should be the only thing happening in the world right now. Because it is yours."

"If I didn't know you preferred women, that might be a matter for debate."

"Oh, be quiet, Troop. Or don't. You can keep talking. I don't hear you. But you need to hear this. One of these days you're going to look at the top of the stairs and expect to see me walking toward you, and I will not be there. Do you want that to happen?"

"Who's put these words in your mouth? Mary?"

"No, Troop. I'm not isolated anymore."

"You don't have any friends, Maureen."

With a small smile, she told him, "I know you can't stand correction. But you're wrong. You have no idea how wrong you are. Where have you been? This house is full of women. They come and go like nothing you've ever seen."

Thirteen

I had fifty reasons why nothing bad would have happened to Mamie and Zollie's boys, but an awful feeling that something had. If they were well, I needed to let them know that regardless of what my uncle had told them, Maureen would welcome them back and increase their wages to reflect the amount of work they did, which she intended to decrease by hiring additional help. One of the maids across the street had a sister moving to town in January, and she would be looking for work.

Maureen had written the directions to Mamie's house, but after driving out there, I saw only a note stuck to the door: "Anybody—Go to the church."

I called Maureen from a filling station to get the name and location of the church and drove there, where I found the minister and his wife behind the white shotgun building, boiling germs out of choir robes in a cast-iron pot, stirring the water with boat paddles. When I introduced myself and asked whether they had heard anything, the wife stomped inside worldlessly, and the minister replied with more anger than I was comfortable for a religious man to express, "You don't know? Maybe you don't. Maybe it is that you simply haven't heard. Zollie left a note on your door late yesterday evening. He was afraid to go in the house."

"I didn't see any note." Trying to deflect his anger, I added, "The house doesn't belong to me. You could say I work there also."

"Well, you're doing all right if you're working now. Some people have to bury the dead and are not able to be so fortunate."

I asked him to explain, but all he would say was, "I went over to Mr. Ross's house early this morning to explain the situation myself, but when I asked for help for Mamie and Zollie, he said the colored community must have him confused with a charity organization."

"You have to believe me when I say I knew nothing about this, and neither did Mrs. Ross. This is contrary to everything she's trying to do for them. If she had seen the message, I can tell you, you would not have gone through such an insult. You would've left with whatever was needed and more."

"That may well be," the minister said, "but I have people

falling over dead out of my pews, which is more of an affront than anything Mr. Ross could say to me. I've ceased to care what people like that have to say. I can't care and do my work. But Mamie and Zollie did need the help, and it shamed him to ask for it and then have to have me go over there on his behalf. When that didn't work, I asked Mr. Ross for the note, which he was happy to give me, and I brought it back and put it on the vestibule wall, where people ask for and leave donations for various things. When he told me I ought to take up a collection for my own kind, I thought how all this church does is trade money back and forth between individuals and families. It isn't ever any new money in the congregation, just the same few worn-out dollars, circulating around from the mother to the midwife that delivers her baby, from the midwife to the grocer, from his widow to the undertaker, and back on around again."

I gave him what was in my purse. He thanked me for the money and asked what my husband did to earn money like that. I told him, "Nothing. Not a thing. But I need Zollie's note, and I'd thank you for showing me where it is."

I went through the sanctuary, where clusters of women were bleaching the wooden pews, and found the long note tacked onto the side of a basket attached to the vestibule wall. It took a while to find it among all the other notes and baskets on this one wall that funded the birthing, medicating, educating, marrying, and burying of an entire community. At first glance, it was hard to make out Zollie's note, which read:

Plez holp fernish my fambly for the grave Mr. Ross

and holp me by a barral soot for my boys and sum stokin
to put on my susters fete. She has turbal col fete. The boys
nevr got the new play thing I promissd and I had to bern
the blankt Miss Morene giv them. I wont them so bad to
have a toy and a nuther blankt.

The boys wuz the lite of my life and Mamie holp them
all like a anjel and then she wonted to lay down and die
wit them. I preshate it all and I no for a fack thay will tell
God you holp.

Just tho me in a dich I aint worth the trubbel for run-
nin off and leevin them wit my moron suster. Im gon git
them baryed and then go jump in fron of the evnin train
Mamie sed it was fine wit her.

I diddent waist my pay. I WONT YOU TO NO THAT. It
was spensiv the chiltren bean sik. I jus wont you to no I am
not lyin and it is gone to take six mons saved pay to giv
the undertacker.

We can com back to work in a week if you will hav us.
We will work dubbel to pay off the det.

Zollie

PS
if you let me also bory sum of yo influez and see if you
culd mak the wite church peoples toll the bell so that my
fambly gits in too hevin. The colort church duz not oan a
bell toar.

> *Plez ask him to ring it 2 time for the chiltren and 1 for*
> *my suster if you dont mind. It is the leest I can do now to*
> *holp them be safe insid the hart of the Lord.*

I took down the note. They were not going to need the church members' help, no matter how willingly it was given. Just before I left, the minister came over and told me that Mamie had been taken to the hospital a few hours before for an injection of something to calm her. "Zollie," he said, "is whereabouts unknown. Mamie had been inviting him to make good on his plan to lie down on the train tracks."

He told me where the children and Zollie's sister were. They were "stranded" at the funeral parlor. The only colored undertaker in town was looking after them, but he was apparently too overworked to even collect the bodies in a timely manner. Rather than bear the tormented delay, some families were returning to the rituals of the last century and taking care of their own at home and burying them in the yard. The city council had, a few days before, forbidden public assemblies, specifically reducing funeral services to small, brief gatherings by a grave. But no matter how modest an effort Mamie and Zollie made, they still had three people to care for at once, and the undertaker wanted cash before he started.

"What are Mamie's plans, exactly?" I asked.

"If Zollie could have gotten the help yesterday," the minister explained, "everything would have gone along fine, but now the undertaker is not able to proceed. He ran out of credit with the casket people. He only went to the house and picked them up as a favor to me. I think Zollie might have gone around to see if he could find some money from somewhere. My wife took Mamie to the hospital and stayed with her there as long as she could, but then she had to go on to the next people." He excused himself, saying that he had three graveside services that afternoon, and he also wanted to see Mamie—"over by the death hospital." He took my hands in his large, dry palms, and told me, "You have a big afternoon ahead. You let me send my daughter to check on your aunt so you can go on and start taking care of things in your uncle's outstanding automobile. I imagine he's not aware that a female's driving it. How much do you think they ask somebody to pay for one like that?"

"Enough to birth and bury everybody in town. Why not let me take you where you're going?"

"Greed and gluttony are twin evils, but yes, I'll let you carry me over to our cemetery, just this side of downtown, about five, six blocks behind where you're staying. And I thank you. Just be careful driving."

I thought he wanted to be sure that neither the car nor the two of us were harmed, but when he added, "A wreck would draw more notice," I realized that he was simply afraid to be seen with a white woman. He was risking his career, his home, and his personal freedom by doing something as uninteresting as getting a ride to work. A minister and community leader was forced to think ahead and see himself being interrogated about how he had seduced and impregnated me, or attacked and impregnated me, on the way to the cemetery.

"I'll take responsibility for having you in the car," I told him.

"Thank you," he said. "Let's hope it doesn't come to that."

As I drove, he told me what had happened at Mamie's house. When the first signs of illness appeared, Zollie frantically bought every grade of medicine that could be had without a medical consultation. They were all dangerous alcohol-based concoctions of everything from tar-wine lung oil to cocaine to morphine. The only difference among the bottles were the designs on the labels. If there were warnings, he couldn't read them. Mamie was alarmed at all the medicines and would not give the first dose of any to the two boys, who were coughing and falling into choking spasms. Frightful dark mahogany splotches were starting to come through like stains on their necks and faces. Mamie prayed that they signified an uncommon but treatable rash. She could not drive, so she had Zollie take her into town to locate a doctor they could drag back out to their house; she made Zollie's sister swear that she would not touch the medicine. It took Mamie and Zollie hours to find even an off-duty nurse who was willing to discuss going to a colored house in the country, but she had her own situation at home and decided not to make the trip.

Mamie and Zollie were gone the whole afternoon, and when they walked back in, the air in the house was thick with death. Mamie stood in the center of the room and screamed until her throat bled. Zollie broke the two back windows to let the sound and the scent out. The two boys were in the bed they shared, in a corner, and their aunt, a girl of about nineteen, was lying under the kitchen table. It looked as though she had crawled there to hide from what was happening to the children she'd been charged to watch after, and from Mamie and Zollie. Empty bottles of patent cures were scattered around her body. The minister said that if the girl had given the boys even a small dose of what was in the worst of the bottles, it was enough to kill a child ten times over. She was not the brightest girl, he said, but she was exceptionally tenderhearted, and when she saw what she had done to her nephews, she apparently drained as many bottles as she could before she lay down and died.

I trusted that the minister's daughter would check on Maureen, as he asked her to do before we drove away from the church, and once I dropped him off at the gates to the colored cemetery, I drove to the depot. The newspaper had reported that undertakers had run out of both the room and the means to keep coffins stocked on their premises. One undertaker's wife had been forced to keep bodies on her dining room and sewing tables. A circus had gotten to town and erected its tent just as gatherings were banned, so an enterprising lumber company was using it as an open-air showroom for the single model of pine box it was selling. That was it—one box, in a choice of three sizes, for fifteen dollars. Rich and poor were in the tent together, but no one seemed to notice or care. The crisp air and the smell of the timber reminded me of picking out pumpkins and Christmas trees with my grandfathers.

Coffins were stacked to the pitched top of the tent, guarded by an armed young man who appeared to be congenitally slow. He had extra bullets in straps slung across his chest, like a bandit, and he carried himself with a sad swagger that would've been sufferable on some other occasion, but not now. Perhaps in exchange for being allowed to fire his weapon at the end of the day, he was making sure that thieving mourners didn't walk off without paying. After the selections were marked with chalk, the purchaser was given a ticket, and went to pay at a table on the other side of the tent. The coffin could be taken wherever the buyer needed it to go, by any one of the many colored men idling at the sides, waiting to be chosen to make a delivery. They shuffled about like children awaiting selection for a team. I knew without looking too closely that Zollie was among them. He had come there to earn the money for his own family's coffins by carrying those of others. I finished my business, buying the three coffins and arranging for their delivery, and then I approached him and asked if I might take him to the hospital to see Mamie.

"I'm still afraid of her," he said. "I wouldn't mind going on home. Coffins don't weigh that much without somebody in them, but they still weigh."

"I know. I'm so sorry. How about if you go over and sit with Maureen for now. Would that do as well as home? Maybe Mamie will feel like leaving the hospital later, after she's had some rest."

He nodded, and so I drove him to Maureen's. The fact that he was a servant attached to the Ross household made his presence in the car acceptable, but I could tell that he was concerned that he wasn't the one driving. I thought of how far removed this hateful trivia was from everything he had had to manage that day, but he couldn't count on the people we passed to offer him any dispensation for the deaths in his house. He was a man whose children and sister had needlessly died, but that wouldn't stop anyone from saying he was also "the nigger who let that white girl chauffeur him like he was owed something." For the second time in one day I had to tell a responsible and capable grown man that I would protect him. That both men were so serious about needing me proved what kind of absurd power was to be had in a mere five feet of white skin.

Zollie nodded his thanks, but said nothing until we got to the house and he knocked on Maureen's bedroom door and asked whether she minded a visitor. She came to the door, embraced him, and told us both to be still and quiet. She pointed to Mamie, asleep in her bed, beneath silver satin. "Mamie just showed up here on foot. I put her underneath the covers," she whispered. "She was mumbling something about how they don't call that place the death hospital for no reason. They sedated her once, and she got some sleep, but when she heard they were going to give her a second shot, she got dressed and left."

"What time is Mr. Ross due to be home?" Zollie asked.

"I'm not sure, and right now, I'm not so sure I care. Mamie explained everything that happened with the note, about the minister being sent away, before she fell asleep. Nothing like that will ever happen again. I am so sorry about your sister and the boys. They don't make words for this."

Zollie nodded. "I appreciate it, and I want to say how glad I am to see you standing."

"Thank you, Zollie. I may have all kinds of hidden capabilities. What I want you to do is go and sit with your wife and listen for the bells. The rector told me to let him know when he needed to ring them. I can call him now, if you want, and let Mamie wake up to that."

"Yes," he said. "Thank you. Yes."

The next afternoon, Maureen and I walked to the cemetery and watched Mamie and Zollie bury their dead. Although she would say only that she preferred to walk and stretch the burning muscles in her back, when I watched her moving slowly down the sidewalk, her eyes straight ahead, I remembered how my mother had declined the ride from our house to my father's grave, saying, "Thank you, but my family will walk. It would be indecent to be conveyed today."

The minister who had helped me prayed over each of the coffins, and then his two grown sons lowered them into the ground with long leather straps. Mamie saw Maureen standing with one hand in mine and the other on a tree and told her to go back home, she should not have come. "The graveyard is too full of disease for you to be here," she said. "You go on home, and we will be on there directly. Mr. Ross isn't there to worry about, so go lie down."

He had gone to Durham on urgent business after I left the note from Zollie on his bed. He'd come into Maureen's room and told her, "I have to leave for a few days, and I wanted to let you know that you should not expect any more roses. My generosity has taken about all it can stand. I am so disappointed in you and your pet that I am truly speechless, Maureen. It is beyond anything I can say. And Mary, cowardly putting that indecipherable note on my bed leaves me with no choice but to think that you're not planning to cease this underhanded behavior. I think that when I get back, we should go ahead and make plans for you to leave."

"I've already stopped your roses," Maureen told him. "But listen to me. Mamie's children have died. I have a baby due in what feels like five minutes. Does any of that mean anything to you? Are you able to just put it out of your mind?"

"Besides having some maudlin encounter with the two of them, who I understand through the rumor mill are due to begin working in my home as though nothing ever happened, there is nothing I can do. As for the baby, I'll be back before then. I'll be gone two or three days. You seem more than adequately staffed with Mary here, and there's a doctor who can be called if anything happens before I get back. You wanted a baby before the operation. You're getting one. While I'm away, you should consider how I feel to be put through an ordeal over something I've not heard one word of thanks for in almost nine months."

"I'm sorry," she said. "You probably didn't hear me."

"When? What do you mean?"

"That night, Troop. You went on so loud for so long, begging me to forgive you, that when I did eventually have something to thank you for, I wanted to hurry the matter along, before it was too late."

"Is this enjoyable, Maureen? Are you getting some kind of pleasure out of saying these things to me, about me? What kind of person are you to be so hurtful?"

"No, Troop. I'm not enjoying it, which makes me wonder why you chose such a malignant hobby. I don't know how anybody can spend so much of a life doing something that feels as terrible as what I just did."

"And you need to let Mary know that not a word of it was true."

"Fine, Troop. I'll do that."

When he was gone, Maureen said, "The night was worse. He cried. He made me promise that if I had a baby, I wouldn't leave him out. I promised, and no sooner had I done it than he got mad and said I'd hidden the Vicks."

"What? Why?"

She put her finger under her nose and said, "Here. He would put a tad here. Just a dot. Enough to keep down the odor of my body, my sex. He said it 'wafted.'"

"That's life, Maureen. I think that's what life is."

"I know. And I was about to say I know that now, but I knew it all along." She hadn't been smiling, but she did as she told me, "It always reminded me of the Delta after a rain. I liked it."

When he was gone, she felt free to roam the house. Although she reported herself to be fifty pounds heavier on her feet, there was a certain lightness about her.

But when we left Mamie and Zollie and were walking out of the cemetery gates, she lurched forward and grabbed on to the wrought iron as though she could easily pull the massive structure to the ground. I made her sit on a stump, telling her I would run home and return with the car, but she was determined to walk. "This baby," she said, "is pushing a foot through my throat. I want to go home, but I need to walk and tamp her down a little."

We took the route that cut diagonally through the town square, and in doing so, we came upon a prophet. He had drawn a small crowd. I couldn't tell whether his chief intent was for them to be converts or customers, but he would've had more to work with had everything downtown except one market, the banks, and the post office not been padlocked. We knew his name was Arthur, because it was scrawled on a sign he held at the end of a long stick. He had several such signs. When he put one down, he picked another up. His running theme was that we were going to die and go to hell if we did not immediately do what he commanded. It was all a question of options, of bliss or torment, of when and how, whether we would be whipped to death by storm winds that evening or die next week in a frenzy of fever.

Maureen said that the last time she had seen him he was offering roofing services, and the time before that he was cleaning gutters. "When Mamie asked him how he could do any of this with no visible equipment, he declared himself so proficient at both trades that it was nothing for him to use his bare hands."

Maureen didn't hire him, but she wasn't surprised to see him profiting from this atmosphere, which was perfect for any instigator who was, as she said, "lazy and alert at the same time, and very, very quick on his feet."

Arthur circled the group, ranting and waving his signs. Neither of us was sure which war could've left him with his particular awful affliction. His eyes were not properly in their sockets. Rather, they were smeared down onto his cheeks, making his expression like that of a person caught in a very sad and painfully frustrating misunderstanding of what someone is struggling to explain to him. That he survived the distance from the battlefield to his pulpit and retained the self-assured, albeit insane, single-purposefulness to condemn a gathering of strangers so vehemently for ignoring the warning signs of a plague was remarkable.

Maureen found a bench and sat down. She couldn't quite reach her back, so she handed me a round stone she had picked up by her feet. While I rubbed the stone hard into what she described as a hot nerve in her spine, we listened to Arthur lay the bulk of the blame for the flu epidemic on self-absorbed people who had ignored the signs right above their heads and concentrated their minds on world domination and the glorified dollar. "People," he screamed, "are irresistible to germs on account of the war has sucked up their nerve power. Bald prophecy of hell on earth came and went unheeded, and now we reap the whirlwind!" Something in his voice, the way it was crazed but also businesslike and even merciful all at once, reminded me of my mother's dire frustration with my brother's daily hangovers, how she would begin stripping his bed with him in it, then harangue him while she scrambled eggs and then while he sat up eating them on his fresh sheets.

Arthur pointed to the clouds and indicated the malignant configurations that he said had been howling about for weeks. Maureen and I followed the line of his arms, and although we did not see the crowned Jehovah on his throne, surrounded by what Arthur was now describing as a sort of peeved, fractious harem, we nodded along with the others when he asked if we had. We stayed a little longer, until Maureen grunted hard, lifted her arm, and said, "Let's go, Mary. Haul me up out of here. I may be too dumb to see what this man sees in the clouds, but I know when I'm having a baby."

Fourteen

I got her in bed and called the doctor. I was told he would be there as soon as he could, but she was moving through things so swiftly that I knew he would never get there soon enough. The minister had a telephone, so I called and asked him to look for Mamie and bring her over. I had collected and set out the emergency supplies that she had put in the closet in case something like this happened. I sat by Maureen and held her when she struggled and when she rested.

Since all she wanted to have ready was the bird's-eye for the diapers, there wasn't anything more to do, nothing outward, at least. Watching her, bending close to wipe the damp hair back from her face, I had a sense that forces were assembling inside her that had nothing to do with anything I'd ever experienced. Her pores were pushing out an odor I recalled from a creek bed I used to go down to with a glass jar to be filled with water for science class—clean but old and mossy. She was perfect.

"You smell like the Delta after a rain," I told her.

"How do you know?" she asked, just as the next contraction was starting. And on the other side, she said, "I'm sorry. That sounded mean. I don't have enough left over to be nice. But everybody knows how the Delta smells."

I had barely enough time to tell her that the odor was in the same category as the lunatic optimism of women, something you can half dream, half remember from a place you've only heard about and somehow be, right before she shouted, "Hush. Hush it. Now." Then she reached up and pulled my head down by her face, kneading the psyche knot, saying, "Breathe. Now. In my ear. Splitting open. I wanted my mother, God damn it."

As she worked through that jagged pain, I was close enough upon her body to feel and hear the surging of all the elements that had been gathering and doubling, the blood and the sheer force. So very much had been taken from her that it made no logical sense that she had enough of what the prophet had called nerve power not to have collapsed after the first contraction and announced that the baby would have to stay inside her indefinitely. Of course, her behavior had been more forthright lately, but it had enervated her just as much to stand up against her husband as it did incessantly to concede. I thought of all the cavalier or premeditated encounters that had tired her mind, body, and spirit, the ones I had witnessed, the episodes before my arrival, the beatings with those hospital towels, the electric currents shot through her. I had to stop myself from saying aloud, "A million other women are giving birth right now, and I know they've survived the same and different dangers, but where did they store up the power and life to form and then urge out a baby?" I was awestruck by the reservoir that had managed to swell within her, and although I loved her dearly and believed I knew her well, I had not known it was there. Foolish young women like me, I decided, can't take excellent notice of what ultimately matters in life because we don't know what it looks, feels, or sounds like, and it takes the wisdom of time and experience to be able to stand out after a rain and divine our own bodies.

Judith Stafford, my mother and grandmothers, and Maureen were women I wanted to be. Their bodies were their own ground, real, wet, dry, hot, cold, vibrating, and still. I kept as much of my body against Maureen's as her writhing would allow, and soon the expanse between my accustomed place as a woman and the ground I wanted to own began to diminish. By the time I had apologized for being incapable of taking away the pain and heard her say, "No. You're taking the pain with me, the weight of your body on me," the life I was living was the one I wanted to live.

I had always heard of the miracle of birth, but the real miracle and mystery seemed to be that this terrifyingly magnificent occasion could just slip into the routine of a woman's life. I had never heard women ask for gratitude from their children for having suffered this ripping pain for them or request special treatment from their husbands. I had never heard a woman on a streetcar tell a man, "I went through childbirth three times. I deserve your seat." And I hadn't heard my mother or grandmothers talk about what was expected of a woman at this moment, how much she would be made to give. I didn't think they were protecting me or that they had forgotten. It had merely never been a part of any feminine conversation I'd heard. Perhaps, I decided, women go through it and go on. They make up the bed and go and do the rest of the day.

Maureen blew out a long breath and said, "There my husband goes, Mary. Out of me. He has nothing to do with this. Off me. The weight, him, is gone."

Mamie entered with a wonderful sense of prerogative and command, shouting out loud, "What's all this crying for? It's just a baby, ladies!"

Maureen got herself up on her elbows. "I've been dying, Mamie."

"I know you have, and it's going to be that way for a while. Let me see how long a time we're talking about. You stay right with her, Mary. This might feel unusual."

Maureen was alarmed, "Unusual?"

"Don't worry, I was telling you how it felt when it was done to me. Okay, here it is."

Maureen closed her eyes, while I watched Mamie's face. She asked about the timing of the contractions, how they had started, whether they had remained even. She raised her head and laid it against Maureen's knee, and with one hand under the sheet, she told us, "Wide and high. The baby's pushing hard and then slipping back up high enough that we've got time to get the doctor over here." Maureen shook her head, but Mamie told her, "You have been like a sister to me, and you know I want to bring this baby into the world, but Zollie and I just lost so much. As soon as this water breaks, you'll have a baby in very short order, but either God or the doctor's going to need to do it."

Maureen was moving into another contraction, and I spoke for her. "So Mamie, she can't have you deliver this baby instead of the doctor because her husband would make you lose more than you already have?"

Mamie stood and wiped her hands. "It isn't just Zollie and me. Mr. Ross would never let her forget that she didn't call the doctor and keep everything the way he wanted it."

"Do it! Break it, Mamie!" Maureen shrieked. "I already said this has nothing to do with him."

Mamie picked up a sterile crochet hook and lifted the sheet. "I'm glad to see you finally out of patience, but you did not see this in my hand. You saw nothing. And when I do this, we're going to have a baby pretty fast now. You two understand?"

We nodded, and then I felt a pleasurable, warm soaking at my knees, up to my hips. Maureen smiled softly and said, "That's nice," before she was thrown into the last of it, where one pain, I thought, didn't have the dignity to stop before another one started. She had no relief.

Mamie said, "Now, now it's crowning," then shouted at me, "You better leave now, go." I told her that I would stay there, that nothing would make me leave, and she spit the words at me, "This is hers. Get out."

I wondered whether this might be some custom from some small corner of the country, and so I left and stood outside the door and listened. The moment I listened and heard nothing, I knew that Mamie had sent me away out of respect for this sacred, horrible time. And when I opened the door, Mamie was leaning over Maureen's stomach, lurching and struggling, trying to cut the cord from around the infant's neck. It was futile. The child was lifeless, blue, a girl. Mamie tried to blow life into her anyway, and only when Maureen said, "Thank you, Mamie, but no more. Let her rest," did Mamie place the baby in her mother's arms and then lie down beside the two of them and weep.

She was whispering, pleading, "It was the cord. It wasn't me breaking the water. You have to know."

I went around to the other side of the bed and lay on the sliver of space by Maureen. I reached over the baby and found Mamie's arm, slick with blood, and told her not to worry. "I found my children that way," she said. "You know I wouldn't have made a mistake. You know that." As I pressed my face into Maureen's ear and whispered, "We'll all be fine," she began such a violent shaking that I had to catch the infant before she bounced out of her arms. I thought she was having a seizure, and worried her teeth or jaw would break. She'd lost so much blood, so rapidly.

Mamie jumped up and pulled a mohair blanket from the top of the closet. "She's freezing. Get this on her. All over.

And then we need to stay on her. All over. We have to bring up her thermometer."

She made me understand that I needed to wrap the baby in the bird's-eye she had been hemming. "Wrap her good. She's cold."

Mamie looked at me, and I knew I needed to ask Maureen whether she comprehended what had happened. "The cord was around her. Maureen, she wasn't alive. Do you know that?"

"Yes. Still cold, though. She can be cold."

I got several lengths of fabric and lay them out beside her, and then lifted the baby from her arms and wound her around and around. I handed her back to Maureen. Mamie quietly asked if Maureen wanted to be bathed now, if she wanted to move to another bed in another room. "No, I'm good, and I need to be here."

"Then do you want me to open a window? It's very close in here."

"No, Mamie. I want it close. I don't want the air to move. This is what it is. But Mary, I do want you to send word to my mother while I rest some, please. Tell her I named the baby Ella Eloise. Tell her you love me. She needs to know. Tell her Mamie took care of me. She needs to know that, too."

When I telephoned the wire office, the clerk told me that there was a telegram from Mississippi waiting to be delivered to my uncle's office. I asked him to read it aloud to me and then send it to the house. Maureen's mother had said, "Thank God you're not dead, but walking wounded is not living. Go and do, Maureen. Live."

My uncle had to be told as well. I telephoned his office and started the process of looking for him in Durham. When I reached him, he assumed he was being unnecessarily bothered, and so I gave him adequate time to listen to himself and then told him that the child was stillborn, a girl. He was silent, and then he said, "Tell Maureen to give her my mother's name."

"No," I answered, "Maureen already named her Ella Eloise."

"And I suppose Dr. Morgan did everything he could." He brushed past the news.

"No, it was Mamie, and yes, she did. It wasn't safe, or even possible, to call the doctor. And Maureen is resting and fine for now. Everything happened more quickly than expected."

"Tell her that I'll be back as soon as I can get things together here, probably early in the morning." His tone was that of a man inconvenienced by an unanticipated automobile malfunction. The only credit I could give him was that he was not attempting to feign the appropriate emotion. He was too selfish to grieve or empathize, and there was nothing in his voice to say he was distracted by the fear his child may have felt while she was strangling. He told me how and when to consult a list of men that included a lawyer and a second doctor, as though some official documentation were needed for the death that the three women who had been in the room were incapable of conveying. He thought he was shifting people around their various stations, and he was happy to stay gone while emotions were spiking and blame for them was being passed around like butter at a table. He was never spiritually here, and I could not think of a time when we were all so grateful for his absence.

Sometime during the night, Mamie lifted the child from Maureen's arms. Her breasts had ached and poured. The swaddling was soaked through with milk, so Mamie dried the child and wrapped her in the remaining length of bird's-eye. Then she took her downstairs to meet the doctor, who, like Mamie, had not changed his clothes in some time. He said it looked as though about one in twenty people who developed bronchial symptoms were dying. The news that her children had been poisoned by the patent medicines had reached him, and he told her that he hoped it would help to know that this tragedy would go a long way to making store owners ban those products from their shelves. She said that she was sorry, but it was no consolation at all. As he examined Ella Eloise, he talked with me about the funeral arrangements; everything could be handled with a minimal amount of involvement, he said. My uncle had spoken to him about "things pertaining to the cemetery plot and things of that nature and so forth," morbid unpleasantries that I was apparently too delicate to manage, despite my having walked through a maze of stacked coffins under the circus tent. But I wasn't offended, as I had been by my uncle's brusque direction that the women in the house be relieved of these hard responsibilities, for the doctor's offer to intercede arose out of respect rather than contempt. He was kind, quietly chivalric. He treated us the way his mother had trained him to treat women, as had my uncle.

While the doctor was filling out a form, Mamie held the

baby. She looked over his shoulder and said, "Dr. Morgan, the other day when I found my two boys, their mouths were full of something like a whipping cream, and I put my mouth to them and drew it over into mine. My husband washed them, and the two of us laid them in the coffins that Miss Oliver here stomped around that terrible tent and bought. Yesterday, she and I delivered this baby. I don't have to tell you what that looked like. We appreciate your kindness this morning, and we're going to take advantage of it on account of Mrs. Ross upstairs needs help, and I'm not feeling so well myself. But we handled these last few days and had to fight death with our bare hands, so we could go talk to the funeral home man. It would not be a problem."

"Yes, she's right," I told him, not knowing what I could add. Yet I had to let him know I agreed with everything she had said. Any colored maid saying these things to a white doctor was at risk and put herself in line to be characterized as an "uppity nigger." I told him that we were making the choice to accept his help, which was different from needing it. Making the distinction obviously meant more to us than it did to him, as he said whatever we wanted to do was fine. He finished up with the infant and wrote Maureen a prescription for laudanum before he examined her. We waited for him to come downstairs and give us a report, but when he returned he only lifted his hat from the banister and told me to tear up the prescription he had given me. "She's fine," he said. "She refuses to take anything. Someone from my office will be in touch shortly."

By then, the death of an infant, even from an elite sort of family, wasn't extraordinary. When the bells tolled that day, we had to decide for ourselves which belonged to the baby. After the men came over with the small white casket, after they placed a wreath on the door, Mamie said she and Zollie were going. She said that she hoped I could understand that they needed time for themselves. They had wanted to go back to the cemetery and had not done that yet. I told her that I understood, and so she went to find Zollie where he had secluded himself in the pantry. "Let's go tell the boys good night, Zollie," I heard her say. "Let's go sit with them awhile."

When I saw how the men had arranged the living room, how they had set the coffin between two tall mahogany chairs, I thought of how these rooms had appeared to me when I first walked into them, how it looked as though someone had created scenes to impress, awe, and perhaps even belittle people who stood there and knew they would never know what it was like to live like this, to be this lucky. But the finality of that white box in the picture should've been all the proof my uncle needed that he would never be able to order perfection. When he came through the door, his first instruction was that things be changed to accommodate guests. Maureen had already given me a note to place on the front door, thanking people for their kindness in honoring the family's need for privacy. She was not going to share her grief with people in the community who had shared nothing pertaining to her life except whispers and lies during the years she had been among them.

I told Troop that I was sorry about his child, and that I hoped he understood Maureen's need be to alone. He said he would deal with his wife, though he wanted to let me know that no one had the right to ban people from his home. He stood and watched me open the door and tack the note up. He stared at it, saying nothing, and then closed the door. Following me, he asked whether Maureen had been able to rest and whether she had required any treatment or medication from the doctor. When I answered to his satisfaction and told him I had drawn her a bath, he said, "It sounds as though you have everything handled. I have some things to do in the study. I'll be up later."

As he walked through the living room and past the coffin, I saw him stiffen. He stopped and turned, as if he wanted to tell me something, and then walked on. All during the night, I had been anxious about his arrival, and I wondered whether this might be the time he decided to correct himself, whether he would allow the baby's death to pass for hitting bottom. I wondered whether he would let her death show him that participating even as a flawed human being in whatever the universe had to offer on any given day wasn't so bad a proposition and that he should go ahead and live before it was too late. He was being crowded, at once, with more intimations of mortality than most people encounter in a lifetime, but the lesson plainly wasn't taking.

Fantasy was required to hear him say anything authentic

and straight, without the taint of harmful intent and calcula-
tion. I imagined him coming into my bedroom, telling me
that Maureen had felt feverish, and he was expected to sit by
her and keep a cool cloth pressed to her brow, but I needed to
do it instead. He would say, "It is more than I can bear. I would
look weak and possibly on the verge of losing control. I do
not like the woman, certainly not enough to look after her. I
want to look after myself. And that is more important than
ever now that my mother is not here to love me uncondition-
ally. I'm the only one left who'll do it. All of you want me to
do these things to earn your love, but it matters not a whit
whether I help her today or not, because there will be something else expected of me tomorrow, a smile of encourage-
ment, a kind word, an arm around the shoulder. It is too
much to ask. There are always conditions placed on me. I'm
expected to show emotions that embarrass me, but the rest of
you seem to have them in abundance and have no difficulty
speaking of them. I'm supposed to look at a beautiful wife
who loves me and feel joy, I suppose, or some sort of deep
happiness. That's a tremendous condition. Her willingness to
show her weakness and joy, everything she feels, frightens me
on one hand and accuses me on the other. So venturing outside of myself truly isn't possible, not today, not ever."

When I went into her room, she was pushing the packs of
ice Mamie had made for her down into her robe. She looked
up at me and said softly, "These breasts haven't been told yet."
The love and awed respect I felt for her were overwhelming—
I could not fathom why he had dismissed her from his heart
and mind, and I was glad that I had been raised by people who

would not think it an immoral or despicable act that I had taken her into mine. We pressed enough milk out to give her some relief, but not enough, we hoped, to make them think that they were finally being put to work. Her breasts were as hard and round as the globe on her husband's study desk, but when I told her she should rest now and dress to sit by the baby later, she said she could manage to do both if we wrapped a scarf around her to secure the ice.

As I was winding the long violet scarf underneath her uplifted arms, she said, "This is like the Hindu levitationist with Mrs. Stafford." After I helped her put on a loose dark-brown blouse, she sent me into her closet to find a skirt that wouldn't hurt in the waist. She sat on the bench at the foot of her bed and regarded the stockings and shoes on the floor beside her, calling out to me that bending over would not be possible for a while. I called back that I would be there in a moment, and when I came back into the room, I saw that she was trying anyway and that her husband was watching her from the door.

She was wearing the brown blouse and her underthings, and her hair was down. When she heard him, she pushed her hair aside and told him that he didn't need to stand there, that he was welcome to come in. She was kind but not afraid, as though years of raw hurt and been coated with a balm, one that made the hurt disappear not forever, but just long enough to get through this day. I was unaccustomed to seeing her with even this temporary relief, and so was he. His heart was breaking at the sight. He turned his head to the side and said, "I'm sorry. I didn't mean to intrude. I only came in to tell you that some people have come and left food, and to see if you were all right, and you are, so, well, I apologize."

He still had his head to the side and was pulling the door closed. In the largest act of either mercy or torment I've ever seen, Aunt Maureen told him to hold it a minute, and she went to the door, closer to him than was needed, and said, "Troop, our baby was strangled by the umbilical cord, and she died. My insides are still on fire. I am throbbing. But I'm alive, and I am so grateful for the pain. I'm grateful for all of it. And I've been thinking about my body, what I shall and shall not have done to it. So you will not take me any-where and have me strapped down and have any of it taken from me. Enough has been taken."

"What are you doing, Maureen? Back up. Why are you so close?"

"Smell me. What's that odor? Listen to me breathe. Can you hear the air? This is how closely you've stood up against me and spoken all these years, nobody but me hearing you. Do you know what it feels like to be this near someone who despises you?"

I was standing by the closet, holding the skirt. When I heard him whisper, "Maureen, please, just let me touch you. Here," I stepped forward. But it wasn't necessary.

She lifted his hand from her hip and gave it back to him, as I had seen him remove her hand from his coat that first evening when she was in the foyer, frightened and needy. "You bitter bitch," he said. "Move and let me get out of here."

"Troop, I'm your wife. But I'm confused. Do you want to hit me or take me to bed? Which?"

"Neither."

"Good, because that's the way things are. Don't you ever attempt to touch me again."

"Maureen, hear me out. I didn't mean anything I said like that. You take everything the wrong way. Let's lie down awhile."

"Oh, Troop, wouldn't it be nice for you right now if you had never humiliated me? I'd have my mother here, helping me get dressed."

He interrupted. "I can help you."

"No." She looked to me standing at the far side of the room. "I have someone who isn't going to pound gratitude out of me for hooking my dress. She's not going to say I'm disgusting. She's not going to hold up a glass and frighten me into saying I see something that was never there. So go ahead. You have all the time in the world you need for yourself today. We're fine here. But thank you, Troop. Thank you so very much. I'm sure the offer counts for something, but if you think I would invite you to help me with my stockings so that you can remind me of how cheap you thought I looked at your mother's funeral, maybe I would need more treatments, because I would be completely out of my mind."

He was able to turn on her before he blinked. "You should have some respect," he said. "There is a child lying in a coffin downstairs, and he has a mother up here half naked with her lamentable whore."

I walked toward them, but she lifted her hand to stop me as she said, "*He* has a mother? She, Troop. And now you need to get out. You need to leave."

Fifteen

I thought I had stopped loving my brother, but as I watched and listened to my uncle, I would think of Daniel with something that I was not quite comfortable calling respect. Respect is not generally given to someone who has killed himself, but I began to see the honesty in Daniel's descent to the bottom. The choice he made once he got there was horrific. By killing himself he escaped his pain, but he admitted it at the same time. Dead, he was nonetheless shouting to the people who opened the door and found his body, "This is how I feel. This is how terrible it is. This is all I know to do." Had my mother gotten to him in time, there would've been another chance for him to tell someone about his agony while he was still available to be loved and helped.

My brother finally said he had had enough, yet my uncle was insatiable. His stubborn and willful lack of compliance with the most ordinary moments of a day, when love is naturally given and received, his willingness to take his wife along as a hostage on the miserable journey of his life, made it impossible for me to forgive him. There was a truth in my brother's death that my uncle would never know. After Maureen told him that she was up against the wall of her endurance with him and would go no further, he understood her to mean that she now intended to live. And he was right. Her child died, and she lived.

Maureen's mother had said the only thing someone could do in the face of such an invincible enemy was to walk away from the field. Rumors of an armistice in Europe were being reported in the newspaper. A false one was declared, but Maureen had declared her own, and she was determined to let her husband know that it was real. It didn't matter whether he kept fighting her or not. He was no longer of consequence in her metamorphosis.

The rector came by to talk with us about how the funeral service should proceed. Maureen had slept beside the coffin all night, and when she staggered a little on her way to greet him, he suggested that he deal with Mr. Ross so that she could conserve her strength. She jerked her head up and said, "No, he slept at his office all night. I slept here, by the baby. I stumbled because my foot was asleep. I can manage. I have everything written out. Here." She gave him a sheet on which she had worked out what she wanted said at the grave-side, and after he read it, he asked again about what Mr. Ross would like to do, and she told him, in a way that would end the discussion irrevocably, that she had no idea whether her husband would even arrive in time for the service.

She pointed to the mixed flowers, not roses, that Troop had ordered be placed by the coffin and said, "This is as close as Ella's father may get to her today."

If the rector came with the intention of praying, he did not act on it. And he was not out the door long before a telegram arrived from Maureen's mother and sisters. She opened it and read. "Finally, something that makes sense," she sighed. "She loves me, and she loves you for helping me, and she loves the baby and says, 'Do not have another with that man.'"

Mamie and Zollie came late in the afternoon. We ate the food the neighbors had brought, and there was no discussion over whether we would all sit at the same table. But then my uncle arrived, and he told Mamie and Zollie to carry their plates to their eating porch, on the other side of the kitchen.

"They are fine where they are," Maureen told him.

"But I want to sit down."

"Then sit, Troop," she shouted, "for crying out loud. We are burying the baby in an hour, just sit and eat a damn meal at the table with the human beings who keep the damn house running."

He closed his eyes, and I could not imagine what he might say when he opened them. Neither could Zollie, who broke the silence. "Mrs. Ross has had a baby." It may have been the first time I did not hear him say to my uncle, "I don't mean any disrespect . . ."

Troop grabbed the edges of the table. "Yes, and where is that baby now?"

Maureen answered, "She's in the living room, which is where you can sit while we go to the cemetery with her." Then she got up from the table and asked me to accompany her while she telephoned the rector.

"You do not need to come," she told him. "We can do this ourselves." She said that it was fine for him to keep the words she had written, because she knew them by heart. Listening, she reached for my hand. "Yes, I understand that," she told the rector. "Yes, but you see, I think He would listen to us just as well. Yes, and thank you."

When she had hung up, her husband asked her if she really meant to bury the baby herself.

"Yes, Troop, I do. I feel a little of the power of God in me lately, don't you?"

He shook his head. "Two women and two niggers. Hardly God's chosen people." He went upstairs, promising with every step he took to hound her to the grave. "There is such a thing as a response to all these assaults, and I will not take this another minute. I took you out of Yazoo City. I can take you back. Too goddamn worthless to be somebody's mother. Better off dead than suckle an ingrate."

Finally he stopped. As much as she had heard in all those years, to hear his opinions so succinctly catalogued while she waited to bury her child was more than any of us thought she could handle. But she did. She walked toward Mamie and

Zollie, who were cleaning off the dining room table, and asked them to sit down. She quietly asked them what they would do if they did not work in her household. Mamie answered: "Rest, I imagine. See how to live without the boys. Take care of our own house, see what that's like."

Maureen excused herself. While she was gone, Zollie asked me whether I thought they were about to be fired, and I told him that Maureen had said nothing of it to me.

She returned and handed Zollie a check. "Zollie, Mamie," she said, "nobody in this house will ever have to listen to anything like you just heard. I want you to take this money and go and do, live."

Zollie looked at the check and said they could not take it.

"If you think of it as money owed you for everything you did here, I think you can."

Mamie thanked Maureen and asked whether she should gather the few personal things they kept in the pantry or wait.

"Either way is fine with me, but I've learned that there's nothing in this house that cannot be left. It's almost dusk. We need to take Ella and start walking."

As Zollie lifted the coffin, he asked Maureen how she was going to get along in this big house by herself, after I had gone back to Washington.

"I'll be fine," she replied. "I have to be. The cemeteries will be full enough with your babies there and mine."

Mamie smoothed the skirt over Maureen's hips and said, "We all love you."

I opened the door, and Zollie carried the coffin outside into a world that in three more days would be at peace.

Mamie and I put Maureen between us and followed Zollie down the long slope of lawn. The cemetery was a few blocks away. We did not hear him come up behind us, but when Troop touched Maureen's arm, she whipped back as though burned. She asked Zollie to wait.

"Say it," she told her husband. "Say your piece. Say something that doesn't hurt and that one thing will earn you the right to help me take our child to the grave."

He looked at her with slow, red eyes, but although he seemed weak and vulnerable, we knew better than to trust him. Pushed to the edge of this circle, he could still reach in and strike. "Maureen, you can't do this," he said. "Are you so incapable of realizing how this little scene reflects on me? Are you so cruel that you would open me to the ridicule this is going to create?"

"Did you hear me?" she asked. "Did you hear me ask you to say one thing that was decent?"

"Maureen, this situation is out of control. You will go back into that house, and we will do this properly."

"Into a house," she told him, slowly and carefully, "that you remind me I don't deserve to be in every day I'm there. A place I'm too ignorant to appreciate correctly." She paused. "But if you're about to cry out here where the neighbors can see you, maybe you should go back inside."

He squeezed his eyes shut and gripped her arm with one hand, keeping the other clenched in a fist. She shook her head when I moved to peel away his fingers. "What do you need, Maureen?" he pleaded. "What is it that you need?"

"I want the baby not to have to suffer hearing her mother demeaned. I want her to be able to go from the house to the street without being pulled back so I can be hated. I don't want her wondering, not ever, if there is something so wrong with me, something that nobody but you can see, that would provoke the kind of treatment she has to witness."

"Maureen, just stop it." Then he spit out the words: "It is dead. It never had to see its mother for what she is."

"That shows how little you know. You should go back into the house before you're seen. Everybody watches, you know, everybody sees, and if you get caught out here with us, exposing some grief for 'it,' you may never live it down."

He leaned in so close that I could barely hear him say, "You are a perfect bitch, Maureen."

She looked at me and then at him, sighed, and said, "Yes, I am, and if I had been one for as long as you have believed it about me, I would have a row of children standing at my feet, not just the one lying in the box. Ella is asking herself, 'If my father is doing this to my mother when I'm about to be put into the ground by myself, what would I have had to hear said to her if I had lived?' Say one more thing to me, Troop, say one more thing that a child should never hear. Do it, Troop."

He crossed his arms, pressed his chin into his chest, and stood silent.

"Maureen," I told her, "the sun's going down."

"You hear that?" she said. "The sun's not going to wait on you, Troop. How much more of my life do you plan to take? How much more do you think I will let you take? You willfully stand between your child and her grave. That will be enough."

He looked at her with such fury that she took a step back. "Get off my property. Now." He moved toward her, jabbing the words out again.

Mamie and I took Maureen between us once more, and as we turned her toward the street, she whispered, "Let him come."

Zollie picked up the coffin, and we all moved to the sidewalk, Troop at Maureen's back, telling her to leave, so furious that he could not help shouting. When we were half a block away, he was still following, screaming, "Don't you ever come back here. You bitch. You vulgar bitches, both of you. You imperious nigger maid and you lackey. Do not ever come back to this house. Did you ever think it may have killed itself rather than be suckled by a perverted bitch?"

It was so near dusk, with gentlemen now coming home from work, getting out of their automobiles, their wives and children at their front doors or running down their yards to greet them. When we crossed to the other side of the street, several gentlemen took off their hats and bowed their heads and then walked hard toward their neighbor and commanded him to get himself under control before they called the police; their families—nobody, in fact—was going to tolerate such vulgarity. They wanted to know what was wrong with him. Had he lost his mind?

I thought that Maureen might glance back to see him being led to his property, but she did not. She walked to the cemetery, and when we had prayed, when we were through, she kissed Mamie and Zollie good-bye and promised to be in touch with them soon. We watched them walk around the graves, to the gates that would lead them to the long, worn path to the colored cemetery. They were going to sit by their boys awhile.

After we were out of the gates, I asked Maureen when she knew that she could determine the outcome of the scene outside the house, and she told me, "After the baby came, when you and Mamie lay down and warmed me. But I thought about it when Judith Stafford left and drew that new, wide circle around herself. I also thought about it every time you talked about your mother and grandparents. And Mary, don't worry about anything we've left behind. I'm not worrying."

She stopped for a moment under one of the old, un-changed gas streetlamps that the thoughtful lamplighter had crossed over to light out of turn, to make sure, he said, "that the ladies walk safe tonight." She thanked him and waited for him to pass before she unbuttoned the top of her jacket down to her waist and said, "I get to ride all the way to Washington, soaking wet with milk. Isn't that amazing, Mary?"

I buttoned her jacket with her tears dropping on my hands. "You would have been," I told her, "a good mother."

"Yes," she said, "such a good mother, but unless we go faster, I'm going to be a such a good wife. But I made other plans, and so let's grab up these skirts. Take them in your hands. Take up these skirts and we'll fly."

Epilogue

On her daughter's first birthday, Maureen and I placed a simple granite marker in our garden, inscribed with the words she had spoken as Zollie lowered the coffin into the ground.

This child has gone. She was rushed into the arms of grace. She dwells now in the heart of the Lord, which is also in the least of us, where peace and certain joy abide. And one day soon, all of us shall follow, to the holy city above, where the mother of Lazarus weeps no longer.

About the author

About the book

Insights,
Interviews
& More . . .

Read on

Meet **Kaye Gibbons**

In 1997, Gibbons was awarded a Knighthood from the French Minister of Culture for her contributions to French literature. In 2001, she spoke at the Pompidou Center in Paris in what one journalist called, "an act of sustained brilliance." She has read and lectured to sold-out audiences from New York to Seattle. With domestic sales of more than 4.2 million copies and numerous worldwide translations, she was designated "one of the most lyrical writers working today" by Entertainment Weekly *and described by one columnist as, "a genius–Madonna in a black leather jacket," and by another as, "a brilliant woman with old-fashioned star quality, rare."*

©2003 Marion Ettlinger

KAYE GIBBONS was born in 1960 in Nash County, North Carolina, on Bend of the River Road. She attended North Carolina State University and the University of North Carolina at Chapel Hill, studying American and English literature. At twenty-six, she wrote her first novel, *Ellen Foster*. Praised as an extraordinary debut, Eudora Welty said that "the honesty of thought and eye and feeling and word" mark the work of this talented writer, and Walker Percy said, "*Ellen Foster* is a Southern Holden Caulfield, tougher perhaps, as funny.... A breathtaking first novel."

   Ellen Foster was recently honored in London as one of the Twenty Greatest Novels of the Twentieth Century. In 1997, the novel won the Sue Kaufman Prize for first fiction from the American Academy and Institute of

Arts and Letters, a Special Citation from the Ernest Hemingway Foundation, the Louis D. Rubin Writing Award, and other major awards. Now a classic, it is taught in high schools and universities, often teamed with *The Adventures of Huckleberry Finn, Catcher in the Rye,* and *To Kill a Mockingbird.* The book has been widely translated, frequently performed in theatres throughout the United States, and was produced by Hallmark Hall of Fame for CBS, starring Julie Harris and Jena Malone.

Published in 1989, *A Virtuous Woman* also received wide praise in the United States and abroad. The *San Francisco Chronicle* called the work "a perfect gem of a novel." Both *Ellen Foster* and *A Virtuous Woman* were chosen together as Oprah Book Club selections in 1998, leading the *New York Times* bestseller list for many weeks.

In 1989, Gibbons received a grant from the National Endowment for the Arts to write a third novel, *A Cure for Dreams,* which was published in 1991. This novel won the 1990/PEN Revson Award for the best work of fiction published by an American writer under thirty-five years of age, as well as the Heartland Prize for fiction from the *Chicago Tribune,* and other awards. In the novel she used transcripts from the Federal Writers' Project of the Great Depression. For the first time, she said, she "discovered the voice of ordinary men and women as a pure form of art and force of nature" and realized those voices would carry her through every novel she writes. ▶

66 A perfect gem of a novel. 99

—*San Francisco Chronicle*

Meet Kaye Gibbons *(continued)*

When *Charms for the Easy Life* was published in 1993, it became a *New York Times* bestseller and prompted a *Time* magazine reviewer to say, "Some people might give up their second-born to write as well as Kaye Gibbons." This novel, which takes place between 1910 and 1945, in the home of three generations of highly intelligent and forthright women, was filmed by Showtime Productions, aired in October 2001, starring Mimi Rogers and Gina Rowlands. *Sights Unseen* (1995) was also a national bestseller and a winner of the Critics Choice Award from the *San Francisco Chronicle*.

The following year, G. P. Putnam's Sons published her sixth novel *On the Occasion of My Last Afternoon,* "a book of saints, sinners, and sorrows offering much pleasure," said one reviewer. Readers agree that it is "another cause for accolades" and many regarded it as her most brilliant to date.

Most recently, she was invited to become a member of the Fellowship of Southern Writers, a most significant honor. She has received the Oklahoma Homecoming Award and was made a member of the YWCA Academy of Women. She was also chosen to write the introduction to the 2000 Modern Library Edition of Kate Chopin's *The Awakening and Other Stories*.

Her latest endeavors, include working on journalistic pieces for publication and collection, a biography, and the sequel to *Ellen Foster*.

Gibbons lives in Raleigh, North Carolina, with her three daughters: Mary, nineteen; Leslie, sixteen; and Louise, fifteen. ∽

A Discussion with
Kaye Gibbons

Kaye Gibbons recently summed up her philosophy of her success when asked whether she was surprised by everything she has achieved thus far in her career:

KG: I would've been surprised had I stumbled blindly into any of it, scratched a lottery ticket and found a prize that would then take me through the rest of my life. I wasn't "lucky" that the books sold. I wasn't "surprised" to learn that they're also taught in literature classes. That sounds arrogant, but it's not. To be able to write literature that sells takes an almost surreal amount of stubborn persistence; imagination; the ability to forego distractions, such as vacations, men, alcohol; and a willingness to lock oneself in a room and submit oneself to constant, ruthless self-criticism. If a writer is any good, he or she will criticize himself so unmercifully that the reader and the reviewer either have to be misguided or wrong to make too much of a complaint. And there's something almost fun about fixing that deal in place. That sounds arrogant, and it may be. But it'd be more arrogant to subject readers, nice, hopeful people, to two hundred and fifty pages of words I had not tried to perfect, that I'd merely typed, as Hemingway said of meaningless writing. I know when it's being done to me, when clichés are bound or filmed and sold, and I don't appreciate it, the disrespect for this gift of language and for the people we're offering it to. ▶

> **If a writer is any good, he or she will criticize himself so unmercifully that the reader and the reviewer either have to be misguided or wrong to make too much of a complaint.**

> " I love the labor, the sheer manual labor that goes into making these books seem as though they were effortlessly written. "

But getting there, to that lucky, sacrificial place, requires long, long stretches of unbroken concentration and more Diet Cokes than most people can or want to tolerate. I love the labor, the sheer manual labor that goes into making these books seem as though they were effortlessly written. I love what has come to feel like a habit of invention. I go about my days stunned that I didn't waste what Walker Percy called a "knack" for writing.

And there's the grace that comes when I'm in my daughters' presence. I go about stunned that I didn't drop or misplace my children or cause them to be expelled from school for repeating what they learned at home. You see, I live alone with three smart and sober teenage girls—it has taken skill, patience, stamina, and that same kind of "knack." And like this forty-year custom of reading and writing, the girls are a seriously profound, sustained joy.

You see, I love what I do. I raise three human beings, and I do language for a living—it's only as terrifying as it is lovely.

The Facts Behind the Fiction
An Exploration of the Spanish Influenza Epidemic

THE SPANISH INFLUENZA EPIDEMIC of 1918 forms the backdrop of the events of *Divining Women*. The tragedies and triumphs faced by Maureen and Mary are intensely personal and often confined within the home, but for millions of Americans in the year 1918, calamities sprung from events in the outside world as a rapidly spreading disease infected children and adults, rich and poor, and man and woman alike. The timeline below illustrates the havoc the influenza epidemic wreaked upon Americans.

As Mary says in *Divining Women*, "The bells continued their tolling, and people were now wearing masks. Terror that the baby would become sick and die inside her blistered Maureen's nerves so badly that she took to be fact the milkman's rumor that the Germans had somehow poisoned our air. 'I know I'm being unreasonable,' she told me. 'The Germans are just a misguided group of people. But this is too evil to be random, and during a war. Things don't happen like this, not this much sickness and death.'"

March 11, 1918: An army private at Fort Riley, Kansas, goes to the infirmary with a sore throat, headache, and fever. Later that day, one hundred soldiers complain of the same symptoms. At the end of the week, five hundred soldiers complain of illness. ▶

> 66 But this is too evil to be random, and during a war. Things don't happen like this, not this much sickness and death. 99

The Facts Behind the Fiction *(continued)*

July 1918: Officials in Philadelphia issue a bulletin warning of the breakout of a sickness that features symptoms of achy joints, fever, headache, and sore throat.

August 1918: Sailors in Boston begin complaining of the symptoms described above. At the end of the month over sixty people were sick, and many had to be transferred to other hospitals.

September 1918: The acting Surgeon General of the Army, Dr. Victor Vaughn, goes to Camp Devens near Boston and states, "I saw hundreds of young stalwart men in uniform coming into the wards of the hospital. Every bed was full, yet others crowded in. The faces wore a bluish cast; a cough brought up the blood-stained sputum. In the morning, the dead bodies are stacked about the morgue like cordwood." Sixty-three men at the camp die that day.

September 5, 1918: The Massachusetts Department of Health issues a warning to the media that an epidemic is under way.

September 28, 1918: Six hundred and thirty-five people in Philadelphia fall ill with the flu after a parade at which two hundred thousand people attended. The city is forced to close churches, schools, and theaters, as well as other locations where the public gathers.

October 2, 1918: Two hundred and two people in Boston die from influenza.

> ❝ I saw hundreds of young stalwart men in uniform coming into the wards of the hospital. . . . The faces wore a bluish cast. . . . In the morning, the dead bodies are stacked about the morgue like cordwood. ❞

October 6, 1918: Two hundred and eighty-nine deaths recorded in Philadelphia.

October 1918: Eight hundred and fifty-one New Yorkers die in one day.

End of October 1918: One hundred and ninety-five thousand Americans have died from influenza. This is the deadliest month so far in American history.

November 21, 1918: Two thousand one hundred and twenty-two people in San Francisco had died from influenza.

66 This is the deadliest month so far in American history. 99

A Reading Excerpt
Charms for the Easy Life

Kaye Gibbons's masterful novel Charms
for the Easy Life *explores the relationship
of three women—mother, daughter, and
granddaughter—living offbeat lives
without men. At the center of their lives
is their matriarch, the strong, wise, loving
grandmother, Charlie Kate, a self-taught
healer.*

*In the following passage, you can take
a glimpse at the marvelous world inhabited
by these three women, and meet the
remarkable Charlie Kate.*

Already by her twentieth birthday, my
grandmother was an excellent midwife,
in great demand. Her black bag bulged with
mysteries in vials. This occupation led her
to my grandfather, whose job was operating
a rope-and-barge ferry that traveled across
the Pasquotank River. A heavy cable ran
from shore to shore, and he pulled the cable
and thus the barge carrying people, animals,
everything in the world, across the river. My
grandmother was a frequent passenger, going
back and forth over the river to catch babies,
nurse the sick, and care for the dead as well.
I hear him singing as he pulls her barge. At
first it may have annoyed her, but soon it was
a sound she couldn't live without. She may
have made up reasons to cross the river so she
could hear him and see him. Think of a man
content enough with quiet nights to work a
river alone. Think of a man content to bathe

> " Think of a man
> content enough
> with quiet nights
> to work a river
> alone. Think of
> a man content to
> bathe in a river
> and drink from
> it, too. "

in a river and drink from it, too. As for what he saw when he looked at my grandmother, if she looked anything like my mother's high school graduation photograph, she was dazzling, her green eyes glancing from his to the water to the shore. Between my grandmother, her green eyes and mound of black hair, and the big-cookie moon low over the Pasquotank, it must have been all my grandfather could do to deposit her on the other side of the river. Imagine what he felt when she told him her name was Clarissa Kate but she insisted on being called Charlie Kate. She probably told him that Clarissa was a spineless name.

Now, some facts of her life I have not had to half invent by dream. She and my grandfather were married by a circus rider in 1902 and lived in a tiny cabin on the Pasquotank completely cut off from everybody but each other. My grandmother continued to nurse people who lived across the river, and soon Indian women in the vicinity came to prefer her root cures to their own. My mother was born here in 1904. She was delivered by an old Indian woman named Sophia Snow, thus her name, Sophia Snow Birch. My grandmother became hung in one of those long, deadly labors common to women of the last century. After thirty-six hours of work with little result, my grandmother decided she would labor standing, holding on to the bedpost for ▶

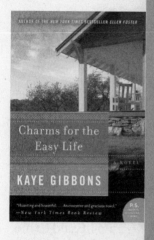

She and my grandfather were married by a circus rider in 1902 and lived in a tiny cabin on the Pasquotank completely cut off from everybody but each other.

support, letting gravity to what it would. Sophia, however, persuaded her to be quilled, and so a measure of red pepper was blown up my grandmother's nose through the end of a feather freshly plucked from one of her many peacocks. My grandmother fell into a sneezing frenzy, and when she recovered enough to slap Sophia, she did. Sophia slapped her back, earning both my grandmother's respect and an extra dollar. Within the hour, my mother was born.

She told me she had a wild-animal sort of babyhood. She remembered the infant bliss of sunning on a pallet while her mother tended her herbs. Her parents kept sheep on free range in the yard, and my mother told me how she had stood by a caldron and soaked the wool down into indigo with a boat paddle twice as tall as she was. She said to me, "We were like Pilgrim settlers. Everything had to be done, and we did everything."

They left Pasquotank County in 1910. The suicide of Camelia, my grandmother's twin sister, made it impossible for her to stay there. They were so bound together that as small children, when they slept in the same crib, they awakened every morning each sucking the other's thumb. Grief for Camelia hounded my grandmother from the place where her family had lived for five generations. Within days after Camelia's hydrocephalic son died, his wildly sorrowful father wandered out and lay like one already dead across the railroad tracks, to be run over by the afternoon train. Camelia lost her mind immediately. My grandmother implored her sister to come stay with her, but she would not. She stayed alone in her

> ❝ She said to me, 'We were like Pilgrim settlers. Everything had to be done, and we did everything.' ❞

house and handled baby clothes and wrung her hands in the clothes of her husband and baby until these clothes and she herself were shredded and unrecognizable. My grandmother would go each day and change Camelia's soiled dresses and linens while she walked all through the house naked, moaning, "Oh, my big-headed baby! Oh, the man I adored!"

> **" She stayed alone in her house and handled baby clothes and wrung her hands in the clothes of her husband and baby until these clothes and she herself were shredded and unrecognizable. "**

Have You Read?
More from Kaye Gibbons

Sights Unseen

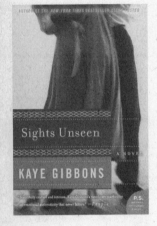

In the days when serious mental illness were described with the crudest of terms and treated with the harshest of methods, young Hattie Barnes lives with a mother who is known around town as the "Barnes woman with all the problems." Hattie and her brother endure the complexities of living with a woman with very little skill for housework and family responsibilities, and even more importantly, for providing her children with the stability and support that they need.

In a lesser family, things could have disintegrated into chaos and despair. But Hattie is blessed with a loving and patient father, who still deeply loves his beautiful but troubled wife, and makes every effort to keep the family together through her turbulent ups and downs of what we today know as bi-polar disorder. And as Hattie looks back at a childhood that was peppered with shame, fear, and insecurity, she is able to see through the clouds and remember the bond that came from the many challenges—a bond that in the end made them all stronger.

"Engaging. . . . Delicately crafted. . . . Kaye Gibbons writes memoirs of other people's lives, fictional people so articulate, so individual that they seem quite real."

—*San Francisco Chronicle*

On the Occasion of My Last Afternoon

Like America in the mid-nineteenth century, Emma Garnet Tate Lowell is at war with herself. She can't help but be affected by her family's wealth and its reliance on the institution of slavery. And bookish and sensitive Emma Garnet often butts heads with her stubborn, self-made father, Samuel P. Tate.

Emma Garnet secedes from the control of her domineering father to marry Quincy Lowell, a member of the distinguished Boston family. When war destroys the rhythm of their days, Emma Garnet works alongside Quincy, an accomplished surgeon. While assisting him in the treatment of wounded soldiers, she comes to see the war as "a conflict perpetrated by rich men and fought by poor boys against hungry women and babies." After Appomattox, Emma Garnet sets out to take her exhausted husband home to Boston, where she begins the long journey of her own reconstruction.

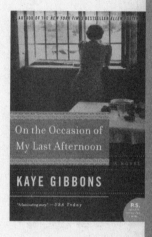

"Haunting. . . . A rare jewel. . . . Kaye Gibbons has gone from being a wonderful, fascinating novelist to a national treasure."

—San Antonio Express-News

The **Web Detective**

www.kayegibbons.com
for more information about Kaye Gibbons

http://www.kayegibbons.com/mailinglist.htm
for information on how to sign up for Kaye Gibbons's mailing list

http://www.stanford.edu/group/virus/uda/
for more information on the influenza pandemic of 1918

http://www.pbs.org/wgbh/amex/influenza/
for information on PBS's groundbreaking series, "The American Experience," and its exploration of the Spanish influenza epidemic

http://www.olemiss.edu/depts/english/ ms-writers/dir/welty_eudora/
for more information on Eudora Welty, whose memories of the Spanish influenza epidemic of 1918 assisted Kaye Gibbons in the writing of this book

http://www.bbc.co.uk/history/war/wwone/ index.shtml
for more information on World War I

http://www.city-data.com/city/ Elm-City-North-Carolina.html
for information on Elm City, North Carolina, where this book takes place

Don't miss the next book by your favorite author. Sign up now for AuthorTracker by visiting www.AuthorTracker.com.